"You were set on running away, is that it? But why, Charlotte? Have I not made it abundantly clear that you are welcome . . . that I want you."

Another rumble of thunder made him pause, so that the words, "I want you" hung on the heavy electrified air. They stared at one another. Charlotte's heart began to pound, and then to beat so loudly that it shut out the sound of thunder, of the river, everything save those words, "I want you."

Without the slightest hesitation, she went into his arms and laid her head on his chest and clung to him.

His lips caressed her hair, her temples, her neck, then, as she lifted her face, he kissed her on the mouth. In that moment, she experienced all the feelings Aunt Lucy had described to her, and more. The world beyond his encircling arms was forgotten: the approaching storm; all the obstacles that lay between them. . . .

ABOUT THE AUTHOR:

Elizabeth Renier, one of England's leading writers in her field, moved into the world of romantic novelists suddenly and with immediate success. *The Generous Vine* won her a scholarship to the Writers' Summer School in 1961, and the Pauline Warwick Award for the best first novel, both given by the Romantic Novelists' Association. She has now written ten books, most of which have been serialized internationally. Her novels have been translated into Danish, Finnish, Dutch, Portuguese, French, Italian and Norwegian. She lives in a converted coachhouse in Exmouth.

THE
SPANISH DOLL
ELIZABETH RENIER

ACE BOOKS

A Division of Charter Communications Inc.
1120 Avenue of the Americas
New York, N. Y. 10036

An ACE STAR Book by arrangement
with the author.

Printed in the U.S.A.

I

The three-masted schooner sped on its way to Plymouth Sound. Many times, during the long voyage, it had seemed to the passengers that they would never see land again. For days on end they had been imprisoned in their cabins while tremendous seas battered the ship, and rain enveloped it like bed-curtains, shutting out all sight and knowledge of a world beyond the bulwarks. But now, incredibly, they were nearing harbour, all danger past.

For Charlotte Endacott, standing in the lee of the wheelhouse, the sight of the English coast did little to raise her spirits. She felt no excitement at the splendid view, now opening out before her, of the port from which her ancestors had sailed for America. The voyage had been too long, too exhausting; and too tragic.

She had set out from Salem, tearfully wished godspeed by her Aunt Lucy, and accompanied by Bella, her old negro nurse, to start a new life. She had not wanted to leave America. But, orphaned and without money, there had seemed no choice. Once aboard, with the sails set and the breeze fresh on her face, she had felt a stir of adventure. That had been seven weeks ago, before she had known the terror of the Atlantic storms, before the poor food and seasickness had sapped her strength. And before Bella died.

Charlotte pulled her grey cloak more closely about her and smiled wanly at a young man who joined her. She had first met John Standish four years ago. She had been fifteen, staying with Aunt Lucy, almost too shy to go to the party to which she had been invited. A dark young man, somewhat older than herself, had asked her to dance and she had been petrified, for she did not know how. He had taught her the steps of the country jig, and soon she was relaxed and laughing. Next day he had sat beside her on a sleigh ride, and again she found herself at ease in his company, able to forget she was from up country, unused to town ways and unsure of herself amongst the pert, pretty girls of Salem. To her regret, he had left for Boston the following day. A week later, she had gone back to Southport, the little community on the coast of Maine whose livelihood depended on fishing. A month after that, her father had died. From then on, life had been so full of hardships and responsibility that all thought of John Standish had been banished from Charlotte's mind. Then, to her delighted surprise, she found he was to be her fellow passenger on the three thousand mile voyage from the new world to the old.

"You must be very thankful that this dreadful voyage is almost at an end," he said sympathetically.

"Yes, indeed. And yet . . ."

He read her unspoken thought. "You are still mourning the death of your servant?"

She nodded unhappily. "I find it impossible to think of life without Bella. And it means I shall have to face England alone. That sounds very weak, does it not?"

He put a hand beneath her elbow. "It is perfectly understandable, especially as I believe you know almost nothing about this relative who is to be your guardian."

"My great-uncle? He is, I believe, a wealthy Plymouth merchant and quite old. Aunt Lucy wrote telling him that I was without parents and she was unable to support me—I did not wish her to do so but she insisted—and he invited me to make my home with him. I do so wonder what he will be like, and if I shall find life in England so very different. Do you look forward to your visit, Mr. Standish?"

He shrugged. "It will be interesting enough, I dare say. As I told you, I am here solely to further my career as a master builder."

She said apologetically, "I am afraid I did not quite comprehend when you told me about that."

He stood with feet widely apart, bracing himself against the movement of the ship. He wore a brown broadcloth suit and a black tricorne. His face was strongly featured, with high cheek-bones and a cleft chin. He was very dark, with black hair and clear brown eyes. A man to lean upon, Charlotte had thought, and she had needed just that. But, after Bella's death, the captain had chaperoned her most strictly, so that she had not seen as much of John Standish as she wished.

"Mr. Roberts, a Boston merchant, saw some drawings I made, and sent for me," he explained. "I have come to England at his expense, to study the best of English architecture—or what *he* considers the best." There was a scathing note in his voice. "Though why we should copy old English buildings instead of developing our own style more suited to a new country, I cannot conceive. Mr. Roberts wishes me to build a school for poor scholars. He wants it modelled exactly upon the one his father attended, a place called Blundell's at Tiverton which is, I understand, an inland town of Devon. In my opinion, he would have done better to send me to Virginia to study the college of William and Mary at Williamsburg."

"How long do you expect to be here?"

"Several months. There are certain towns which Mr. Roberts wishes me to see, besides the Universities of Oxford and Cambridge. At such places I shall see traditional English architecture, he informed me. But I shall take every opportunity of seeking the latest in building design and materials. While he provides my livelihood, naturally I must do as he wishes. But when I have sufficient money to strike out on my own . . ." He broke off, pointing. "That must be the Eddystone lighthouse which the captain spoke about. And there, at last, is Plymouth."

She looked where he pointed and saw, rising from the water, cliffs on which stood a great stone fort. To the left of the ship was a small island.

"Drake's Island," John told her. "I suppose, for those who have a mind for it, this place is full of stories of the past; the defeat of the Spanish Armada, the sailing of the Pilgrim Fathers. For myself, I look to the future. It is my wish to play some part in the shaping of the future policy in the colonies, besides making my mark upon their buildings."

All around them, sailors were busily preparing to enter harbour. Charlotte felt a sinking of her spirits. However dreadful the voyage had been, however nightmarish the days when she had striven in vain to save Bella's life, and afterwards felt so ill that she had not cared whether she lived or died, at least the ship had become familiar to her. The captain and John Standish had been sympathetic and helpful. She had come to know the faces of the crew, and some by name. There was a routine about the days which in itself gave a sense of security. For weeks past, all decisions had been made for her. Had it not been for John Standish, she thought, she might have sunk into complete apathy of body and mind. Even as it was, she was well aware she had never looked so thin and pale, her hair lifeless and her skin roughened by the wind and intermittent sun. She did not look forward to the moment when the ship docked and she would meet her future guardian for the first time, and begin, alone, her new life.

An hour later, she felt even lower in spirits as she bade goodbye to John Standish beside the gangplank leading to the steep, slippery steps of the quay. He had wanted to remain with her until her guardian had been told of her arrival and sent someone to fetch her. But the captain, ever mindful that she had been put in his care, had forbidden it.

"It would not do at all, ma'm," he said firmly. "What impression do you suppose would be formed if your guardian were to learn that you, a young unchaperoned girl, had constantly sought the company of a bachelor who is in no way related to you? No, Miss Endacott, it would be most unwise for Mr. Standish to be seen waiting with you. And I myself should feel I had acted most improperly were I to give permission for him to do so."

John took her hand. "Have courage, Miss Charlotte. You are feeling very low in spirits at present, I know. But it will pass. You will allow me to write to you?"

"I shall be most grateful if you will. For, until there is time for a letter to reach me from Aunt Lucy, it will be my only link with home. Not, of course, that Salem was really home to me."

He pressed her fingers in sympathy. "You have had a great deal of unhappiness. I pray sincerely that the future may be brighter. As soon as I return to Devon I shall seek your guardian's permission to call upon you."

"I shall look forward to that," she said warmly. "You have been very kind. Believe me, that has made all the difference in helping me to retain what little courage I still possess. Where will you go first?"

"To London. The captain tells me there is a stagecoach which leaves Plymouth every day. We have docked so early I shall hope to get a seat on it."

She sighed and looked at him with envy. "You sound so assured, as if already you knew your way about England."

He laughed. "New experiences do not daunt me, Miss Charlotte. You must not let them frighten you."

"I will try not to," she said, forcing a smile.

He left her then. She watched him cross the gangplank, mount the slippery steps of the quay, exchange a greeting with a group of old men dressed in fishermen's jerseys, and stride purposefully towards the town. At the corner of a tall building he turned and raised his

9

hat. Charlotte waved her handkerchief. Then he was gone.

She felt as if the sun had gone behind a cloud. She wondered if he would keep his word and write to her, if he would visit her when his work brought him again to Devon. Fervently she hoped he would, and that her guardian would allow the friendship to continue. And now, perhaps within an hour, she would meet that guardian for the first time. She shivered, then forced herself to recite under her breath the formal speech with which she intended to greet this wealthy great-uncle who henceforth would have charge of her life.

There was much activity on the ship, the sailors busy about their tasks, men coming aboard, shouting greetings and orders. Presently she saw the captain coming towards her. His step was not as brisk as usual, his face was very grave.

As he reached her, he cleared his throat.

"Miss Endacott, I regret I have to impart some bad news. A message has just been brought me by a notary's clerk which deeply affects you."

Charlotte clasped her hands together beneath her cloak. What more bad news could there possibly be? Had she not endured enough during the past four years?

She ran her tongue over her dry lips and asked in a tightly controlled voice, "What news have you, Captain Blankerton? You had best tell me at once."

He glanced down at a note in his hand, cleared his throat again, then looked at her with troubled eyes.

"The message concerns your great-uncle, ma'am. You had better prepare yourself for a shock." He paused, then said in an embarrassed rush, "Mr. Matthew Endacott died, two days ago."

II

In the small, stuffy lawyer's office, Gervase Endacott laid aside his black tricorne and silver-topped cane and, as if it pricked his fingers, took the quill the notary proffered. With equal distaste he picked up the document lying on the desk, and began to read it aloud.

"Plymouth, June 1772. I, Gervase William Endacott, gentleman, of Stokeleigh near Tiverton in the county of Devon, do hereby take upon myself the guardianship of Charlotte, only daughter of the late James Endacott of Southport, in the district of Maine, Massachusetts . . ."

He broke off to ask, "Mr. Melhuish, what makes you assume I am a suitable person to have charge of this girl?"

"You have a large house, sir, doubtless a housekeeper and many servants."

"That is true enough. Stokeleigh is sufficiently large to make over a wing for the girl. But I would remind you that I am a bachelor, without any female relative nearer than the western edge of the county."

"I do not think that is of any consequence. The letter from Salem states quite clearly that Miss Charlotte will be accompanied by a nurse."

"But it does not state her age?"

The lawyer smoothed out a tattered sheet of paper. "Much of her aunt's letter cannot be deciphered, for it has suffered badly from the voyage, as you can see. I can, however, read quite plainly that Miss Charlotte is 'a sweet, gentle child of good intelligence, able to read and write and sew very prettily.' "

"In fact, a suitable pet to amuse Uncle Matthew in his dotage," Gervase remarked sarcastically.

The lawyer looked at him disapprovingly. "You do the late Mr. Endacott an injustice."

"Do I?" Gervase raised his eyebrows. "I have scarcely set eyes on the old fellow these last five years. Which makes all the more puzzling why he should choose me as his sole beneficiary. I surmise you are no clearer on that point than I?"

The lawyer rested the tips of his thin fingers on the desk. "I must admit it did surprise me when Mr. Endacott changed his will. Originally he intended leaving all his property to charity."

"And I can scarcely be deemed in need of that." Gervase laid down the document and went to the window, staring down into the narrow, cobbled street.

The notary permitted himself a closer scrutiny of the young man who had come to Plymouth to attend his uncle's funeral. Gervase's tall, slim figure was attired in well-cut silk breeches and a coat of plum-coloured velvet over an embroidered waistcoat fastened with gold buttons. His fair, curling hair was tied with a wide black ribbon; there were silver buckles on his black, square-toed shoes, and Honiton lace at neck and cuffs. What had possessed the self-made Matthew Endacott to leave his considerable fortune to a young nephew who so obviously did not need it, Samuel Melhuish could not guess. There was but one indication.

He said, "Mr. Matthew did make one remark concerning you, sir, a very strange remark in my opinion."

Gervase turned and asked languidly, "Indeed? What was it?"

The notary cleared his throat nervously. "He said, sir, and you must believe that I am specifically quoting your uncle, 'I hear that my nephew Gervase wishes to absolve the sins of his fathers. I've a mind to provide him with the means to do so, and he can absolve mine as well. And much joy may he have of it.' " Mr. Melhuish paused. Then, as Gervase made no comment, he asked, "Do you understand his meaning?"

Gervase toyed with the quill. "Possibly. Though how Uncle Matthew learned of the matter, I cannot conceive."

And that, the lawyer realised, was all this superior young man would choose to say on the subject. Again he cleared his throat and suggestively pushed the document towards Gervase.

"What *is* absolutely clear is that, by inheriting your uncle's estate, you also become responsible for his liabilities. And his orphaned great-niece is one of them, without a doubt."

Gervase frowned down at the piece of paper which, if he signed it, would lay such an onerous task upon him.

"Have you *no* idea of this girl's age?"

The notary shook his head. "None at all. But the fact that she is to be accompanied by a nurse and not a governess would suggest that she is not above six years old. A child may read and write and sew well enough at that age, I believe. Though, like yourself, I am a bachelor and have little knowledge of children. And now, sir, if you will . . ."

"Oh, very well." Gervase signed his name with a flourish and laid down the pen. "When they arrive, you will doubtless arrange for them to be conveyed to my house at once. Though what my housekeeper will make of it, I cannot imagine." He picked up his hat and cane and made for the door.

"One moment, sir, if you please."

Mr. Melhuish turned the key of the drawer in which he had put the document, and leaned across the desk.

"The fact is, Mr. Endacott, they are already here. The ship, seven weeks out of Salem, docked this morning."

"The devil it did!" Gervase's languid manner vanished. "You knew this and did not inform me at once? There is some trick here, I'll wager."

"There is no trick. I merely considered it advisable

that the matter of the child's future should be settled before she sets foot in England."

"Then, presumably you have been down to the ship and seen the girl? You are hiding something from me, are you not? Something unpleasant?"

Indignantly Mr. Melhuish denied the charge. "Indeed I am not. Nor have I been down to Sutton Pool. But I have sent a message to the captain, asking him to acquaint the nurse with the news of Mr. Matthew Endacott's death, and assure her that suitable arrangements would be made as soon as possible."

"And you have made very sure of those arrangements, have you not? I consider you have all but used methods of blackmail to gain my consent to this guardianship."

The lawyer drew himself up. "May I ask, sir, what else you would have me do? Miss Charlotte, who is, after all, your second cousin, is undoubtedly your responsibility now. And, in any case, to whom else could she turn? Who else in England would give her a home? To travel three thousand miles, believing she will find a welcome, and . . ."

Gervase made a dismissive gesture. "You need not preach at me, Melhuish. You have made your point. Distasteful as I find the situation, I will accept it. I will myself go down at once to Sutton Pool and make the acquaintance of this girl of unknown age and habits. And of her nurse, who will most probably turn out to be a Red Indian with feathers in her hair, able only to communicate by sign language."

Mr. Melhuish raised his thin hands. "Sir, you must be jesting! Miss Charlotte, as a member of your family, will surely have been most carefully brought up."

Gervase laughed shortly. "You have a touching, but misplaced regard for our family, Mr. Melhuish. Tell me, what would you consider a suitable present with which to greet my ward? A game of ludo, or a spinning-top? Stokeleigh is not over-endowed with toys. Childhood, in my parents' opinion, was a regrettable incident in life which should be passed over as swiftly as possible."

The shocked expression on the notary's face made Gervase smile to himself as he went down the narrow stairs into the cobbled street and turned towards the harbour.

With some difficulty he found a pedlar of toys. Cutting short the man's patter, he chose a puppet, a gay Spanish doll decked out in black and red and gold, which pirouetted and curtsied as the toy-seller manipulated the strings. Embarrassed, Gervase paid twice the amount asked and hurried off, thrusting the doll into the deep pocket of his coat.

When he came to New Street he slowed his pace, wanting to delay the moment of meeting this unknown child for whom he had so reluctantly made himself responsible. For once, he wished Sophia was here. Her three sisters were all considerably younger than herself and she was used to dealing with them. The expression made him wince mentally. But it was true. Sophia always "dealt with" people, just like his own mother had done. He supposed that in time he himself would grow used to being dealt with by Sophia. She would deem it to be for his own good, no doubt.

All through his life, everything he most disliked and shrank from had been for his own good, according to his parents: a cold tub even on mornings when the ice had to be broken; being whipped for every slight misdemeanour; learning to box with his two elder brothers; school. It was not until he reached the University of Oxford that he discovered there were other young men like himself, who preferred books to hunting, the skilful play of foils to the clumsy fisticuffs practised by his brothers, the witty turn of phrase rather than the rough jests of the merchants and country gentry who were his father's and brothers' associates. But he had never dared disclose his feelings save to the one person who understood, his maternal grandmother. It was she who had put forward the money, and so silenced his family's opposition, for his years at Oxford and the Grand Tour of Europe which followed.

To his mother, he had been the greatest disappointment. The least likely of her sons to do so, he had been the one to survive. Even now, three years after her death when, contrary to all expectations, he was master of Stokeleigh, her influence was so strong that he was constantly plagued by the self-doubt she had induced in him from his earliest days.

He was certainly beset by doubts at this moment. Had he done right? Was he the proper person to act as guardian to this American child? Would it not have been better to wait a little?

He flicked a cabbage stalk into the gutter with his cane. There had been no choice. The child was here. accompanied only by her nurse. He could not have left them stranded in a ship or in some hostelry in a country strange to them, and quite unprotected. He would take them to Stokeleigh and consult Sophia.

Within sight now of Sutton Pool, he quickened his steps. A three-masted schooner, showing signs of a rough passage, rode at anchor beside the quay. A group of old men, their sea days over, sat on bollards and fish barrels, smoking long pipes and offering advice to the sailors busy about the decks and rigging.

Gervase made his way carefully down the slippery steps, aware of curious stares, and a sudden silence on the quay. At the end of the gang-plank he almost fell over a sailor, on his knees scrubbing the deck.

"My name is Endacott," he said, "and I am looking for . . ."

"That'll be the young lady you're wanting, over there." The man jerked his thumb over his shoulder.

On the further side of the ship, a girl leaned against the bulwark, listlessly looking down into the littered water of the harbour. She wore a grey cloak and, although it was travel-stained, Gervase noted that it was of good material, and the hood trimmed with fur.

She turned as he approached and gave him a look of quick appraisal. His first impression was of a pale, oval-shaped face, the plainness of which was relieved only by the intensely deep blue eyes. The girl's hair was tucked beneath her hood, her cheeks and lips were without colour. There were dark shadows beneath her eyes. She looked forlorn and dejected and much too young to have sole charge of a child on so long and hazardous a voyage.

"I am sorry you have been kept waiting," Gervase said. "The news of my uncle's death must have greatly disturbed you."

"Your uncle? You are, then . . . ?"

"Gervase Endacott. Charlotte is my second cousin. Perhaps you will be good enough to fetch her, so that I may . . ."

"Fetch her?" the girl repeated in a puzzled tone.

"Why not?" Gervase asked with equal perplexity. "I assume you have left her below, in your cabin, while you waited for news." It occurred to him that his ward must be an unusual child if she did not wish to be on deck, staring at all the new sights and the ships. He asked anxiously, "She is not indisposed, I trust?"

When the girl did not reply, but stared at him as if he had made the most outlandish suggestion, he repeated, a little impatiently, "Come now, I pray you fetch the child. You must both be anxious to set foot on land again after so many weeks at sea."

The girl made no response. Gervase realised that he had not made his position clear.

"I am sorry," he said more sympathetically. "I should have explained that, as Mr. Matthew Endacott's heir, I also inherit his responsibilities. I am now, in fact, Charlotte's legal guardian. It is my intention to take her—that is, to take you both—to Stokeleigh, my house near Tiverton, and I think that we should set out at once."

Uncomfortably aware of the curiosity of the sailors

moving about the deck, he reached into his pocket and produced the doll.

"I bought this for the child, though I am not sure of her age."

As he thrust the puppet into the girl's unwilling hands, she momentarily closed her eyes. When she spoke, it was in so low a voice that he could only just catch her words.

"I fear this will be a great shock to you, sir. But you see, I am Charlotte Endacott."

In the silence following her disclosure, Gervase was aware of the raucous cries of herring gulls, the creak of the ship's timbers, a sailor shouting from the rigging. Before he had fully taken in what she had said, the girl laid a hand on his arm.

"I am so very sorry to disappoint you."

He saw, before she bent her head and the edge of the hood hid her face, that her eyes were filled with tears, and her fingers, which clutched the absurd Spanish doll as if it were a kind of talisman, were trembling.

Although her companion was not hurrying, Charlotte found difficulty in keeping up with him as they went along the quay and began the steep ascent of New Street. Her legs felt odd, as if they were floating some way beneath her body, and she had the impression that the cobbles were rising towards her, then receding; that the buildings were swaying and dipping all around her. She stopped and, leaning against a wall, closed her eyes.

Gervase asked anxiously, "Are you indisposed?"

"It is because I have been at sea so long, I think. I never felt like this after a voyage down the coast on my father's fishing boat."

"How very thoughtless of me," Gervase said at once. "Come, take my arm."

It was better after that. For, although she still felt as if she might fall, his arm prevented her from doing so. He did not speak as they made their way to the hostelry,

and she was grateful for his silence. Her mind still be-
numbed by the news of her great-uncle's death, she
could not yet fully accept the further disclosure that
her future lay in the hands of this elegant, superior
young man who described himself as her second cousin.
Nor could she fail to realise that the discovery that she
was not a child had given him as great a shock as any
she had received. His face as she had told him who she
was, his look of dismay as he glanced down at the doll
he had given her, had very nearly reduced her to weak,
helpless laughter. Instead, she had surprisingly found
herself in tears.

At the inn, while he gave orders to the landlord, she
was able to study him more closely. She had been told
that some of the wealthy planters in Virginia and Mary-
land conducted themselves like English aristocracy, but
in Maine few men had riches or leisure enough for the
luxuries of life. Gervase's appearance, and the smooth-
ness of his hands, suggested that he had never done a
day's work. Yet he was not an aristocrat, she reminded
herself. He was no more high-born than she was, for
they were of the same blood, difficult as it was to believe.

As the landlord led them to a private room, she was
very conscious of the glances which followed them.
Fervently she wished that Bella had been with her.

Gervase said, as the innkeeper left them, "I am still at
a loss, ma'am. You surely did not cross the Atlantic alone?
Mr. Melhuish—he is the notary dealing with the late
Mr. Matthew Endacott's affairs—understood that Charlotte—that is, you," he amended awkwardly, "would
be accompanied by a nurse."

Charlotte sat back in the winged chair so that her
face was hidden from him. She clasped her fingers tightly together and made an effort to control her voice as
she explained what had happened.

"They wrapped Bella's body in canvas," she ended,

"and the captain read the burial service. She was a freed slave, you see, a Christian."

"I am sorry," Gervase said, formally.

She saw the look of relief on his face as the landlord returned with wine and biscuits.

Sipping the wine, she asked, "Did I hear you aright, Mr. Endacott? Is it true that you are my guardian in place of Great-Uncle Matthew?"

"Perfectly true, absurd as the idea must appear to you. For I surmise I am not many years older than yourself."

"I am nineteen," she volunteered.

"And I, twenty-six. Nevertheless, I have signed a document making you my ward in the eyes of the law." He drained his glass and poured another. "It seems the best course is to consult Mr. Melhuish about this new development. The position, as I think you will agree, is an extremely delicate one. I am a bachelor. My mother is dead. I have no sisters. What is to be done, I cannot at the moment conceive."

She bent her head. "It appears I am entirely in your hands. My mother came of a family long settled in America and I know of no relatives of hers in England. On my father's side, my grandfather, as you probably know, had quarrelled with . . ."

"Naturally," Gervase broke in. "He was an Endacott."

She looked up in surprise.

"Did you not know that was a family trait?" he asked. "The Endacotts always quarrel, father with son, brother with brother. Your grandfather quarrelled with his father and sailed for the American colonies. Uncle Matthew left home and made his fortune here in Plymouth. My father . . ." he shrugged and laughed shortly. "My father crossed every man he ever met, I think. Sometimes our family differences have led to honours and riches, sometimes to—fratricide."

Charlotte gazed at him in dismay. "I heard nothing of this. Papa scarcely ever spoke of his family."

"And I have disillusioned you? Shocked you, by your expression. But we are straying from the point. Before I consult Mr. Melhuish, I think it would be as well if you told me a little about yourself."

"My father died four years ago," she said wearily. "There was little money and my mother set up a small school for the fishermen's children in Southport. But she was not strong and she missed Papa dreadfully. When she developed pneumonia in the spring of last year, she seemed to have no will to recover. After her death, Aunt Lucy sent for me to go and live with her in Salem, but she is a widow and takes in sewing to keep herself." Seeing his raised eyebrows she said quickly, "Perhaps you do not realise how hard life is in the colonies?"

"No, I had not given it much thought. It is likely you will find it a deal more comfortable in England." He bowed slightly. "You will excuse me while I go and consult Mr. Melhuish?"

"Of course," Charlotte answered resignedly. "I am, as I said, entirely in your hands, just as if I were the child you expected."

When he had gone she leaned against the chair back and closed her eyes. If only, when she opened them again, she could discover she was dreaming, that the last few hours, indeed the whole voyage had been only a nightmare, and she could find herself back in her little room in Aunt Lucy's wooden house in Salem, with Bella sleeping in the truckle bed beside her.

But when she opened her eyes, she was in the unfamiliar surroundings of an English inn, and the voices beyond the door sounded as strange as those of the Indians who came to trade in Southport. And the walls of the room would not stay still.

When Gervase returned, he did not look pleased.

"I have discussed the matter with the lawyer," he told Charlotte. "Embarrassing as the position is for us both, there would appear to be no way out of it. My uncle's wishes were perfectly clear. Even if I were to renounce his bequest to me, and with it, the responsibilities, that would scarcely be of benefit to you. By your own admission, you have nowhere to go, no one to turn to, in England."

She thought he need not have put it quite so bluntly, but there was no denying that what he said was true. When she made no reply, he went on, speaking in as casual a tone as if he were discussing the disposal of a bale of merchandise.

"In the circumstances, there appears to be no alternative but for me to undertake your protection—at any rate for the present. You are agreeable to that?"

His manner stung her to a sharp retort. "Have I any choice?" Then seeing his mouth tighten, she added quickly, "I am sorry. Doubtless you are being kind. I regret your having to be burdened with me."

"It is no burden, but a pleasure, I do assure you," Gervase said at once, accompanying the words with a charming but wholly artificial smile.

She wanted to tell him to speak the truth, that where she came from, people lived too close to the realities of life to make a pretence of their feelings.

She rose, pulling on her gloves. "Aboard the ship you spoke of setting out straight away for your home. I am quite ready."

Gervase hesitated. Then he said casually, "As to the journey, Miss Endacott, I fear it will be necessary for you to travel in advance of me. There are certain matters which Mr. Melhuish wishes to discuss further."

Neither his words nor his manner deceived her. He had been willing enough to accompany the fictitious child Charlotte and her nurse. He had not the slightest desire to make the journey with the real Charlotte.

"You will be perfectly safe," he was saying with cool assurance. "My coachman and footman are to be trusted completely, and there is accommodation already reserved for me at the Hotel in Exeter, a most comfortable place kept by a Frenchman. You could reach

Stokeleigh tomorrow afternoon and I have given Thomas a note for my housekeeper fully explaining the situation. Mrs. Yeo has been with the family for many years and will place herself entirely at your service." He glanced out of the window. "They are putting your portmanteau on the carriage now."

"But if I am to go in your carriage, how will you travel?" she asked.

"On horseback. Doubtless I shall be able to procure a suitable mount at the livery stables here, and changes can be hired on the way."

It was all so simple if one had money, she realised. Life could be made so easy, all problems and unpleasantness ignored or evaded. For her, and for almost all the people she had ever known, it had been so different.

But she was not going to admit to this superior young man that she had never travelled in a private carriage in her life, nor had any dealings with coachmen or footmen or even housekeepers. Mounting the carriage steps with as much dignity as she could muster, she settled herself in the corner and suffered the impassive-faced young footman to place a rug over her knees although she was quite warm enough. Something hard pressed against her thigh and she remembered that, not knowing what else to do with it, she had hastily thrust the doll Gervase had given her, into the pocket of her cloak.

Gervase gave some final instructions to his coachman, made her a perfunctory bow and went back into the inn. Again, Charlotte yearned for Bella's comforting presence, and at thought of her old nurse, tears pricked her eyelids. She looked out of the window as the carriage made its way through Plymouth, forcing herself to take some interest in her surroundings. The city seemed so big and sprawling, the stone and slate houses so tall and solid after the wooden structures of Massachusetts. People jostled each other in the narrow streets and shouted from windows high overhead. Dogs ran barking beside the carriage. At the street corners sailors stood in groups, laughing and singing.

An urchin leaped on to the carriage step and thrust his head inside, begging. Startled, Charlotte was about to declare that she had no money, when the coachman's whip flicked the boy on the neck and he yelped, falling backwards on to the cobbles. Charlotte struggled with a leather strap and managed to pull up the window. She leaned back in her corner, trying not to be seen, and was thankful when at last the city had been left behind and they were travelling through open country, although she could see little because of the high hedges on either side. The vehicle swayed and lurched so that she might still have been in the ship as it fought its way through the Atlantic rollers, and she was glad to find a plaited cord to hold on to.

At three o'clock they stopped for dinner at an inn, she did not know where. It was the first meal she had ever taken alone. The landlord and the young serving-girl were as deferential to her as Gervase's servants, but several times she caught them staring in curiosity, especially when she found difficulty in understanding what they said. Contrary to her expectations, she found that she was hungry, and encouraged by the landlord, ate well and drank a good deal of wine.

Afterwards, attempting the steps of the carriage, she felt as unsteady as she had on leaving the ship and was grateful for the footman's supporting hand. When she thanked him for his help, he smiled at her. He had a fresh complexion and bright blue eyes, and seemed no older than herself.

"You'll feel better after a night's rest, ma'am," he assured her. " 'Tis allus a difficulty, so I've heard, getting the proper use of your legs after a long voyage."

She dozed on the next stage of the journey, waking every so often as the carriage lurched into a particularly deep rut. At length, since there was no one to see her, she put her feet on the opposite seat and sank into a troubled sleep.

A sudden clamour brought her sharply to wakefulness. They were again in a town, rattling over the cobbles, amongst even greater crowds than before. The people were different, she noticed. Instead of seamen's clothes, a number of men wore military uniforms and others were in the sombre black of clergy.

The carriage turned sharply to the right and passed through an arched gateway into a close, which was planted with elm trees and dominated by a church whose immense size made Charlotte catch her breath. As the vehicle drew to a halt the footman opened the door and offered his hand.

"This be Exeter, ma'am. I hope you'm not too tired with the long drive."

She stood at the foot of the carriage steps, looking about her. People strolled across the grass beneath the trees or stood in groups on the cobbled paths leading to the church. She could not take her eyes from the great church, lit by sunset glow.

The footman followed her gaze. "You'm taken with the cathedral, ma'am? I'm used to it, being Exeter born, but I expect to anyone coming from over the sea 'tis quite a sight."

"I have never seen anything like it. Is one allowed inside?"

"Why, of course." He peered at her doubtfully. "Were you wanting to attend a service? Because, if so . . ."

She shook her head. "No. I had a fancy for going inside, alone—just for a few minutes."

The young man put a finger under his wig to scratch his head. "I don't know as Mr. Endacott would approve." Then, searching her face, he asked hesitantly, "You'm a bit nervous, ma'am, of going into the hotel on your own? You've no need to meet anyone save the Frenchie landlord and the maid-servant who'll wait on you. There's nought to fear, ma'am, truly."

She smiled at him, grateful for his understanding. "You are very kind. What is your name?"

"Tom. Thomas, really, of course, but I like Tom better. If you specially want to go into the cathedral, I'll walk over with you while Benedict goes on to the stables, and wait just outside for when you come out."

"Thank you. I have missed going to church these last weeks, although the captain read prayers and lessons on board ship." Again she was reminded of Bella, and the sailors standing around in uneasy silence while the captain read the prayers for the dead.

Inside the cathedral the setting sun lit up the stone vaulting, shone warmly on the great pillars. There were only a few people there and it was very quiet after the noise of the streets. Charlotte knelt in one of the middle pews. But she found herself unable to recall any of the prayers she had said regularly every Sunday from childhood. She felt a loneliness such as she had never known, not even after her parents were dead; and a sense of helplessness since she no longer had any say in her future. Desperately she tried to remember a prayer of supplication, but no words would come.

Reluctantly she rose to her feet and went out of the cathedral. On the central path a man was standing, his head tilted back as he gazed up at the massive walls of the great church. Charlotte stood quite still, clasping her hands tightly together, not daring to believe her eyes.

The man turned and began to walk away down the cobbled path. Charlotte hurried after him.

"Mr. Standish."

He looked at her in astonishment. "Miss Endacott! What are you doing here? I thought you to be in Plymouth."

"And *I* thought *you* to be on your way to London."

"So I am. But the stage-coach stops at Exeter and so I decided to spend a night here and have a look at some of the buildings Mr. Roberts wished me to see." He looked at her more closely. "You appear distressed. What has happened?"

She explained, somewhat incoherently. Out of the corner of her eye she saw Thomas, waiting anxiously at the end of the path. She supposed he had drawn the wrong conclusions, but it seemed of no consequence. All that mattered at this moment was that her unspoken prayer had been answered and the only person she knew in England, her one friend, had miraculously appeared when she most needed him.

"I—I am so very glad to see you," she said, with a catch in her voice.

He took hold of her hand. "Poor Miss Charlotte. It was monstrous of this man who calls himself your cousin to send you on this journey alone."

"He told me his servants could be trusted," she said lamely.

"Even so . . . Why did he not arrange for you to stay at least overnight at the house of your relative in Plymouth?"

"Great-uncle Matthew had died."

"But only recently, you said. Surely his house was not entirely shut up? I have no wish to frighten you, but I do not like what you have told me. Have you actually seen the document of which Mr. Endacott spoke—the deed of guardianship?"

"Why, no."

"What is he like—this so-called cousin? In appearance, I mean."

"Quite handsome, and most elegantly dressed. He carries a silver-topped cane and speaks in a superior manner. He is not like any other gentleman I have met —not in the least like you, Mr. Standish." She put her hands to her cheeks. "Forgive me, I did not mean to . . ."

"Offend me? No, of course you did not. And I do assure you, I have not the slightest desire to resemble a dandified Englishman."

She said, glancing over her shoulder, "Mr. Endacott's

footman is approaching. He will wonder who you are."

John thrust up his chin. "I shall soon tell him, *and* ask him some questions. Have no fear, Miss Charlotte, I shall not leave you alone in a situation like this."

Gratefully she walked beside him to meet Thomas, her arm held tightly beneath his. Her worries for the moment were over, her fears allayed. John Standish would take charge of her. And never in her life had she felt so in need of someone to lean on, as in this noisy, crowded city with unfamiliar sights and sounds all about her, and the chill of the evening rising from the grass, in the shadow of the huge, overpowering cathedral.

III

Gervase said patiently, "I have already explained to you, Sophia, why I rode from Plymouth in this suit."

Sophia Pendleton tossed her head. "I still fail to comprehend why you could not have hired a carriage, or at worst, travelled on the stage-coach. You must have looked ridiculous astride a horse. Why, you are not even wearing boots."

"It is really of no consequence," he remarked wearily.

Sophia raised her dark eyebrows. "I do not suppose you stopped to consider for a moment my feelings in the matter? Do you think I shall enjoy the stories that will be told of how you trapesed around the county on hired mounts, decked out in velvet and lace, for all the world as if you had come drunk from a ball? Do you think I shall relish my future husband being made a laughing-stock?"

Gervase sighed. Whenever Sophia made reference to their marriage he found himself sighing. If his brother Henry had not been such a fool as to drown himself, and Stephen at the same time, Gervase would have been free to choose his own wife, and it would certainly not have been Sophia. Nor, he knew with equal certainty, would she have chosen him. But they had to make the best of it, for an Endacott-Pendleton marriage there must be, according to the contract made by their respective fathers.

"Regarding this young woman," Sophia was saying, "surely there was some means of avoiding this absurd form of guardianship?"

"There was no way," he answered doggedly. "I assure you. I would have seized upon any means of escape from it, had any appeared likely. I fear she is my responsibility. And what to do with her I have not the vaguest notion."

"Do not be so stupid!"

Sophia flounced across the drawing-room and sat in the window embrasure. The Pendletons' house stood high on a knoll above thick woods. Far below, the River Exe wound like a silver snake through the water meadows. To Gervase, the place was full of charm and atmosphere. Built during Elizabeth's reign, it had been used as Royalist headquarters in the civil war, then usurped by the Cromwellians. The initials of generations of Pendletons were carved in the mellow stone walls, their crest displayed over the porch and on the iron entrance gates. To Sophia, taking over its management following her mother's death ten years since, Highcleave Manor offered no charms. It was, to her mind, a rambling, inconvenient house with too many nooks in which her younger sisters could hide from her; too many staircases, too many draughts. To reach it from the turnpike road was a hot, hard ride in summer, and often impossible in winter. Stokeleigh, built comparatively recently, was much more to her fancy.

She said briskly," You must arrange the girl's marriage at once. Presumably there is sufficient money in your uncle's bequest to provide a dowry for her, since you say she is penniless."

"She has but just arrived in this country," Gervase pointed out.

"What does that signify?"

As she looked up at him, he was aware, as always, of how handsome she was, and of how well she would have suited Henry. She was wearing her crimson habit, her colour was high and her dark hair loosened by a hard gallop across the hills.

"The girl will be delighted to have a suitable betrothal arranged, you may be sure," Sophia remarked complacently. "And I cannot think there is the slightest need for her to go into mourning since she has never met this relative who was to have been her guardian." She hitched up her skirt a fraction and leaned her head against the panelling of the window, so that her clear-cut profile was outlined against the distant woods. The material of her jacket was taut over her full breasts. "Tell me, Gervase, what is she like?"

He rubbed his cheek. "A timid creature, singularly unattractive, I thought. Of course," he added quickly in fairness, "she was doubtless suffering the effects of a long voyage, and the news of Uncle Matthew's death must have come as a great shock to her."

"Dark or fair?"

"I cannot tell you for certain. Her hair was almost covered by a most unbecoming grey hood. Her eyes are blue, that I did notice. But her manner was so—so meek, I suppose would best describe it. In fact, she could well have been the nursemaid I first took her for."

Sophia tucked a loose strand of hair behind her ear and smiled with satisfaction. "In that case, it is likely she will prove amenable to any arrangements made for her future. What age is she?"

"Nineteen."

"Then indeed a marriage must be arranged. Otherwise you will have her on your hands for another two years. Gervase, do not look so vague. You may safely leave the matter in my hands." She rose and said dismissively, "It is time I changed into a day gown."

Walking beside her through the hall, he observed, "The house is very quiet. Are the girls out?"

She frowned in exasperation. "Do you never remember anything I tell you? Catherine and Julia have gone to our cousins in Norfolk, with Papa."

"Yes, you did tell me," he admitted apologetically. "But was Becky not going as well?"

"I decided that the climate would not suit her. The winds in Norfolk are much colder than here and would most probably prove harmful to her chest."

"She must be disappointed. She was looking forward to meeting her cousins."

Sophia said coldly, "It is better that she suffers disappointment than pneumonia."

"Yes, of course," he agreed hastily. "I am not questioning your decision. You have, after all, had the care of your sisters these past ten years. Becky, I think, was only two when your mother died."

"Exactly. And I thought I should never rear her. I had to tell the nurse . . . Why are you smiling, Gervase?"

He regarded her with awed amusement. "You are incredible, Sophia. You could scarcely have been more than a child yourself."

"I was twelve," she told him with fierce pride.

"The age Becky is now. Yet you treat her as if she is still a child."

"And so she is. By force of circumstance I grew to maturity before my time. Rebecca, as the youngest, and being delicate, has always been spoiled."

Gervase had his own ideas of what spoiling a child meant, and they were not the same as Sophia's, but he let her remark pass for the sake of peace.

At the door she halted, tapping her whip against her boot. "Why, I have just remembered something my groom told me. He was riding back from Tiverton, two days ago, when he had to pull aside for a carriage to pass—your carriage, Gervase. There was a man inside, he said, a stranger. I took no notice at the time, assuming you had returned from Plymouth and brought the notary with you, perhaps."

Gervase picked up his hat. "Your groom must have been mistaken. There was no man in my carriage, only the girl."

"I assure you, there is nothing wrong with Tobias's eyesight," Sophia retorted. "He described the man to me, for he had a clear view as the passenger leaned from the carriage window. Very dark, Tobias said, and dressed in brown. Which," she added reflectively, "would certainly, had I thought more of the matter, refuted the idea of his being a lawyer."

Gervase stood frowning down at the polished floor. How could there possibly have been a man in his carriage? Even if the girl had been prepared to commit such an indiscretion, which seemed unlikely, his servants would not have disobeyed his orders. "There must be some mistake," he said again.

Sophia said, too sweetly, "I will call Tobias if you wish."

"No," he said emphatically, "I should not dream of questioning your groom about a matter which concerns Miss Endacott."

"Why not? She is your ward."

He flushed. "The whole situation is quite ridiculous."

"I agree. It is what I said half an hour ago. So you will see that my plan is the only one and you had best leave the matter in my hands."

"Very well," he agreed reluctantly. "But let it be a suitable match, Sophia. The young woman, after all, is a member of my family."

"That is all the more reason why you should enquire into her behaviour, is it not? As, flushing more deeply, he turned from her and mounted his horse, she added, "You should beware of meek women, Gervase. They have means of getting their own way where bolder spirits often fail. For a girl to have a strange man in her carriage on her second day in England calls, I am sure you will agree, for *some* explanation."

It was cool beneath the trees by the river. Charlotte sat on a grassy bank, trailing her fingers in the water. In a meadow opposite, a herd of cows flicked their tails spasmodically at the flies which troubled them. A wagtail ran to and fro on a patch of mud, chasing small insects. It was quiet and peaceful, yet Charlotte could not feel at peace. She was unused to being idle and she was unable to rid herself of the sense of guilt it engendered. Which was absurd, she had to admit, since she had tried her best to make herself useful, requesting Gervase's housekeeper to find her some task in the kitchen, or a piece of mending, or even silver or furniture to polish.

Mrs. Yeo had raised her hands in horror. "Indeed, ma'am, Mr. Gervase would never hear of such a thing. He gave no clear instructions in his note. After all, ma'am, you are of the master's family even though you've come from foreign parts. Just you have a nice rest after that dreadful voyage and later, if you want to occupy your hands, mebbe Mr. Gervase'll send into Tiverton for a pretty piece of embroidery for you to work."

"Embroidery!" Charlotte had repeated to herself scornfully. There had not been time for such niceties in Southport. Between them, she and her mother had spun and woven, stitched or knitted every article of clothing for the whole family. Her father had shot the animals whose skins were turned into breeches and shoes, and trapped the creatures whose pelts provided the fur capes and hats needed in the cold winters of Maine.

But this was a different world. She had only to turn her head to see just how different. The house which she must now learn to call home stood on rising ground above the river, its gardens sloping to a terrace with a low stone wall over which clustered masses of pink roses.

It was a solid building with square windows and a stone portico, flanked by stables and outbuildings. The red brick glowed warmly in the sun. Two weathervanes, which Thomas had told her represented the sheep from whose wool the Endacott wealth had stemmed, scarcely moved in the still afternoon.

Thomas had also told her that the house had been built in the Georgian style some fifty years ago by Gervase's grandfather. It contained a collection of treasures the value of which Charlotte could not even guess: French furniture, Italian paintings, silks from the East and china from Germany.

"The Endacotts have always been lavish in their spending," Mrs. Yeo had said. "Not Mr. Gervase, though. His favourite room is the library. A great one for his books, he is."

Cautiously Charlotte had questioned the housekeeper and footman about their master. Their answers had been similar.

"A bit strange in his ways, but there's none of us would say he's not a good master to work for. Keeps himself to himself, more of a scholar really than a country squire." And Thomas, who had been in Gervase's employ only a year, had added, "Not a bit like his brothers, by all accounts. Proper young rakes they were, so I've heard, given to hunting and shooting and fisticuffs, and they did a good deal of wenching around the district too . . . Oh, I beg your pardon, ma'am, I shouldn't have said that."

But that piece of information gave Charlotte the opportunity she wanted.

"Mr. Gervase is different in every way, you said?" she enquired casually.

"Oh, yes, ma'am," Tom answered eagerly, relieved that she had not been offended. "You'd never find *him* chasing the maids or taking the village girls behind the haystacks. A bit afeared of women, I think he is. But then, if you'd met Miss Pendleton . . ." He broke off, colouring. "There I go again, letting my tongue run away with me. Still, perhaps 'tis as well, for I'm think you'm a mite feared of the master, and you've no need to be."

She had reported this conversation to John Standish, for John, to her relief and pleasure, was but a few miles away, in Tiverton. He had altered his plans completely, and for her sake decided to make a plan of Blundell's school as the first of his commissions, so that he might be at hand should she need him.

He had ridden over on the previous day to tell her he had found lodgings in the town, that he had seen the school and it might well take him several weeks to make as exact a copy as his employer required. This news had raised Charlotte's spirits, and given her back some measure of self-confidence. She supposed that when Gervase Endacott returned home, she would be obliged to ask his permission to continue her association with John. For the present, she was content to take pleasure in his company without the slightest qualm.

At a sound behind her, she started to her feet. Despite the housekeeper's assurance, she could not rid herself of the idea that danger might lurk amongst the trees or in the undergrowth. Although the Indians around Southport had been friendly, their sudden, silent emergence from the woods had always frightened her. She found it difficult, also, to believe that there were no longer any dangerous wild animals in England.

Seeing Thomas approaching, she laughed at her unnecessary fears, and went to meet him.

"The master has returned," he told her. "He wishes to see you, at your convenience."

"I will come at once. Where is Mr. Endacott?"

"Up there on the terrace, ma'am," Thomas told her, holding open the little gate which gave on to the river path. "He'll see a difference in you, if I may make so bold as to say so."

"Indeed?" She spoke coolly but the young footman was not so easily put off.

"You'm looking that much better than the day you came ashore. Proper peaky and downcast you were then."

His words confirmed her own opinion. Only this morning she had looked in her mirror and not felt dismay at what she beheld. Her hair had been washed, and hung in soft brown ringlets on her shoulders. The colour had returned to her cheeks and lips, the brightness to her eyes. She believed she had already put on weight with the excellent food which had replaced the poor fare on board ship. Her few gowns had been pressed by one of the maid-servants and she had chosen, this June day, a simple blue one with elbow length sleeves and a soft, frilled neckline. Her appearance, she was well aware, would not equal that of the stylish ladies with whom Gervase was doubtless used to associating, but at least she no longer looked like the bedraggled waif she must have seemed at their first meeting. This knowledge lent her confidence to assume an outward composure even though her heart was beating fast and her hands felt cold.

Gervase came along the terrace to meet her. He was dressed in a grey suit almost as elegant as the one he had worn in Plymouth, and his fair hair shone in the sunlight. As he greeted her, she was gratified to see a swift change of expression on his face, his eyes widen in obvious surprise.

As he hesitated, she spoke first. "I hope you did not have too tiring a ride."

His assured manner returned. "Thank you, it was quite pleasant, since the rain held off. Judging from your appearance, I need scarcely enquire if you are recovered from your long voyage. You have, I hope, been taking advantage of the weather to rest out of doors?"

"I have been sitting beside the river. But I find it so difficult to accustom myself to leisure. From early childhood I have had constantly to be employed with one task or another."

"Your father was not pioneering in the wilderness, surely?"

"No. But life is still hard, even on our part of the coast which has been colonised for many years. Papa fished for cod off the Newfoundland Banks. We had a small piece of land for cultivation. We kept a cow and some pigs and poultry. My mother worked very hard, although she came from a home in Salem in which there had been two servants. She was not strong but she had great courage, and after Papa died she set up a small school. Perhaps I have already told you that?"

He made a dismissive gesture. "And you helped her?"

"I did what I could."

Charlotte was not prepared to tell him how she had cut wood and fetched water; how she had dug and hoed, planted corn with dead fish as fertiliser, a task which had taken all her determination.

"Could not your mother's family have helped you?"

"Mama married against her parents' will. She was too proud to appeal to them."

Gervase drew forward a garden seat for her, then persisted with his questions.

"When your mother died and you went to Salem, life was a little easier?"

"A little. But my aunt, as I mentioned, was not well-off." She turned to him impulsively. "Mr. Endacott, I think it is next to impossible to make you understand. Your life and mine are so wide apart."

"Yes, I realise that. Yet I am not without some knowledge of how the less fortunate live. There is much poverty in Tiverton and the surrounding district. Less than a mile from here, in the village . . ."

"I walked along the river bank yesterday and came to the village. But everyone stared at me, so I turned back."

"The villagers are naturally curious," he said, smiling. "The sight of a stranger, or in their words, a 'foreigner,' is quite an event."

"I did not think I looked so very different from an Englishwoman."

He made a slight bow. "You look very charming this afternoon, cousin Charlotte."

She flushed, embarrassed by the unexpected compliment, and said hurriedly, "I noticed some cottages by the weir. They seemed very near the water."

His mouth tightened. "They are too near it. Whenever the river floods badly, it reaches the lower floors. So far there has been no actual danger, but if Sir William Ransom carries out his plan of constructing fish pools on his property, and diverting the course of the river, it will be a different story, I fear."

"Do the owners of the cottages know this?"

"They belong to me. I own the village and all the surrounding land. As far as you can see, up and down the river, across the river, behind the house, every tree and blade of grass, every animal and bird and fish, is Endacott property."

She said, in surprise, "You sound as if that fact displeased you."

"It does."

"But why? Surely it is a splendid thing to own land? It is what all men in America seek to achieve."

Gervase rubbed his forefinger along the rough stone of the parapet.

"It is not the actual ownership which I abhor. It is how property is acquired that matters. And the way in which our family has acquired its wealth is something of which I am ashamed, not proud." He glanced at her, hesitated a moment, then said, "It is as well you should be warned of the reception you will be met with in Tiverton when you admit to the name of Endacott."

"Warned?" she repeated in dismay. "Why should that be necessary?"

Gervase sat on the low wall and swung a mauve-stockinged leg. "There have been merchants who made fortunes out of kersey in the town and gave back some of their wealth. Men like Peter Blundell who founded a school; or John Greenway who built almshouses and spent a deal of money on St. Peter's Church; and many more. The Endacotts have taken all and given nothing. They have squeezed the lemon wholly dry and drunk every drop of the juice. And left behind a trail of starving children, ramshackle buildings, misery and—hatred."

The word, spoken quietly, sounded to Charlotte all the more alarming.

"If this is true," she said tentatively, "and you feel it should not be so, surely you have the remedy? Why do you not endow a school or build some almshouses? Why do you not distribute charity where it is needed? If you are as rich as you said . . ."

"I did not say I was rich," he corrected. "I said I owned a great deal of property."

"Is that not the same thing?"

He tucked in a trailing rose stem. "I was the third son and by the law of primogeniture could expect nothing from my father. Now, by the deaths of my brothers, I am left with everything. But my hands are tied by the terms of my father's will. Every transaction is made, every decision taken, by my agent in Tiverton. Being a man of my father's choice, he will not agree to raise wages or effect any improvements to the tenants' homes."

Gervase had laid aside his air of languid elegance. His hands were clenched and he ground his heel into the gravel.

"So the injustice continues," he said grimly. "The hardships and grievances are ignored, as they always have been."

"I still do not fully understand," Charlotte said apologetically. "Even if you cannot control such matters, is there anything to stop you bestowing charity where you wish?"

"Nothing at all, save the lack of any sum worth the giving. Even my income is prescribed, like a schoolboy's pocket-money."

"What was your father's reason for such stringent conditions?"

For a moment he looked as if he was not prepared to answer. Then he shrugged. "Because he knew only too well what I would do, given a free hand. You will think me a disloyal son, no doubt. But my father and grandfather represented everything I most abhor. They bequeathed me a legacy of injustice, and I have been powerless to right it." His manner changed, and he smiled at her. "It will be different now, though, thanks to Uncle Matthew's bequest. I can bestow charity where it is most needed, make what improvements I wish, and all with Uncle Matthew's blessing. And my agent may go to the devil. Why, cousin Charlotte, I could even buy you all the gowns and jewels you have had to do without."

"I have never coveted such things," she told him.

He laughed. "You have the makings of a Puritan, perhaps? In any case, I surmise 'twould be more sensible to provide you with a generous dowry so that we can find you a suitable husband. In fact, I dare swear Sophia already has the matter in hand."

The words were like a physical blow. Colour flooded into Charlotte's cheeks and she turned quickly away, making a pretence of smelling the roses.

"I had not realised the matter was one of such urgency," she said, striving to control her voice.

"There is no immediate hurry," Gervase assured her loftily. "But I think you must agree, 'twill be quite the best solution to the problem."

"The problem of your being forced to accommodate me in your house?"

He seemed taken aback. "I did not mean to cause you any offence. As we have already agreed, the situation is a delicate one. I am a bachelor . . ."

"So you told me," she said, facing him again. "We are also agreed, I believe, that I am your second cousin and

40

your ward. I cannot see that my presence here can place the reputation of either of us at stake."

"Well, no, but . . ." Frowning, he shredded the fading petals of a rose. "The fact is, I myself am to be married—one day."

"I see. I do not wish to appear unreasonable, Mr. Endacott, but I have been in this country less than a week. I had not expected to be sold off quite so soon."

Gervase dropped the rose and stared at her, horrified. "Sold off! I' faith, you must not use such an expression. Surely it is the practice in America to arrange marriages? Why, my own was contracted between Sophia's father and mine some years ago."

She was so upset she could not stop herself saying bitingly, "Then you have been somewhat tardy in fulfilling the contract, have you not?"

Gervase's eyes widened and he gulped inelegantly. Charlotte felt elated at having shattered his air of superiority, and shown him that she was not the ineffectual creature she must have seemed to him at first, willing to have her life settled without question. That he had treated her differently this afternoon, that he had taken her into his confidence and aroused her sympathy, rendered so much more hurtful the disclosure that his one idea was to rid himself of her as soon as possible.

She said recklessly, "I have reason to believe it may not be necessary to trouble yourself about my future. Given a little time, I am confident I may well be able to arrange matters for myself."

Gervase rose from the wall and moved towards her, a hand outstretched. "Cousin Charlotte, I beg you . . ." Then, abruptly, his tone changed. "What did that remark signify?" Before she could reply, he went on, "Cousin Charlotte, there is a matter I wish to discuss with you. I prefer to question you rather than my servants. Perhaps you will be good enough to tell me if you travelled alone in my carriage from Exeter?"

She had been about to tell him of John Standish. Instead, she exclaimed furiously, "And if I did not, will you have me tied to a whipping-post to improve my morals?"

There was another startling change in Gervase. He caught her wrist and she was surprised at the power of those slender fingers. He stood over her so that she was forced to tilt her head backwards, which hurt her neck.

"Do you realise what you are saying?" he demanded. "You are implying that you invited a stranger into my carriage—for on your own admission you know no one in England. Presumably, though I did not suppose you to have any money, you bribed my servants to disobey my orders. Apart from any danger to your person, you laid yourself open to the most harmful gossip. Altogether, it seems, you have behaved as if . . ."

Charlotte wrenched herself free and struggled to her feet, her cheeks flaming. "How dare you! Without even waiting for an explanation, you damn me out of hand. You told me in Plymouth that our family were known for their quarrelsome natures. I believe you now. For it has taken an Endacott to make me angrier than I have ever been in my life."

While Gervase regarded her in dismay, she turned on her heel and walked swiftly along the terrace. She heard him hurrying after her, calling on her to stop.

"If you would explain," he pleaded as she gained the doorway.

She turned, thrusting up her chin. "The time for that is past. You may find out the truth from your servants. And when you do, *cousin* Gervase, I hope it affords you as much humiliation as you have just heaped upon me."

Thomas stood in the doorway of the library, clearing his throat. Gervase did not look up from the book he was reading. Or pretending to read, Thomas observed. For, illiterate though he was, he could not fail to perceive that the volume was being held upside down.

He tried again, more loudly. Gervase glanced up, frowning. "What is it you want? Out with it."

"Mr. Standish is here, sir, asking if he may pay his respects to Miss Endacott."

"And who, pray is Mr. Standish?"

"The American gentleman, sir, Miss Endacott's friend."

Gervase turned a page of his book. "I was not aware that we were favoured with any American gentlemen in the neighbourhood, Thomas."

The young footman said doggedly, "It's the one who arrived two days since, with Miss Endacott."

Gervase's fingers tightened on his volume. "Where is he residing?"

"In Tiverton, sir," Thomas answered. It was not usual for his master to be so dim-witted. He explained patiently, "Mr. Standish is the gentleman we brought from Exeter. Doubtless Miss Endacott has told you about it, for I assured her that in the circumstances you'd not take exception."

"*You* assured her!" Gervase laid aside his book. "Since when has it been your prerogative to undertake . . . ?"

"Begging your pardon, sir, I don't understand that word."

"Then I will put it more simply. Am I to assume that you took it upon yourself—you and Benedict, that is—to allow a strange man to travel in the carriage with my —my ward?"

"He wasn't a stranger. He was well known to Miss Endacott, though meeting him in Exeter gave her a proper surprise."

"So they met by chance?"

"Why, yes, sir, in the cathedral close."

"And may I ask, after the very careful instructions I gave you, how Miss Endacott came to be alone in the cathedral close?"

"Well, she . . ." Thomas put a finger under his wig to scratch his forehead. "Surely she's told you of this, sir? 'Tis true, I did leave her for a few minutes, while I went into the hotel and gave the note to the Frenchie, like you said. But 'twas all perfectly innocent. Even if I did wrong, Miss Endacott didn't, that's for sure."

Gervase raised his eyebrows. "You are quick in the lady's defence."

"Yes, I am, sir," Thomas said truculently. "Proper at a loss and low spirited she was before she met Mr. Standish. If you'll permit me to say so . . ."

"I do not permit you, Thomas. You are over-free with your opinion as it is. But to continue with your story . . . Miss Endacott and this—this gentleman having assured you that they were known to each other, you then assumed him to be a fit associate for her and invited him to ride in my carriage next day? Is that it?"

Thomas's wig moved up and down as he scratched his forehead to aid concentration. "Yes, sir, that's about it. We didn't think we were doing wrong, Benedict and me. We put our heads together, and . . ."

"That will do, Thomas. You may send this gentleman in to me, and, when I ring, request Miss Endacott to join us."

When the library door closed behind his footman, Gervase threw down the volume of essays at which he had been staring unseeing for the past half-hour. Why the devil hadn't he questioned the girl more tactfully, made her realise he was only concerned for her good? She was young, new to England, probably completely without experience of the type of man who hung about quiet, innocent-seeming places like the cathedral close. Yet Thomas had said this man was well known to her. Was it likely? With America three thousand miles away? And with all her talk of poverty and the narrow life she had led, was it probable that she would know anyone with sufficient money to travel to England? And yet . . . The fellow had actually come to visit her, here at Stokeleigh, was even asking permission to do so.

This was all Sophia's fault, Gervase told himself irritably. If she had not been so free with her gossiping tongue, if that damned groom of hers had not been at such pains to report what was none of his business . . .

The young man who came into the library was scarcely what Gervase expected. He was dressed in a brown suit, plain but of good quality, and his linen shirt looked equally well cared for. He crossed the room with a firm stride and there was certainly no evasion in the lively dark eyes.

He accorded Gervase a formal bow. "Your servant, sir."

Gervase's acknowledgment was no more than courtesy demanded. "Pray sit down, Mr. Standish," he invited in his coolest tone.

The visitor sat down squarely in the big leather chair, his feet planted firmly on the carpet, his hands clasped between his knees.

"Now, Mr. Endacott," he said, "there are one or two questions which I should be obliged if you would answer."

Gervase, leaning back in his chair, one mauve-stockinged leg crossed over the other, raised his eyebrows.

"Indeed? Then we appear to be at some odds, sir. For, since this is my house and Charlotte is my ward, it would seem more fitting that I should do the questioning. In fact, Mr. Standish, I consider that your conduct, and my ward's, call for an immediate explanation."

When Charlotte entered the library, she found John standing before the fireplace, feet apart, hands clasped behind his back and an angry expression on his face. She hesitated in the doorway, then quietly closed the door and went to him.

"Mr. Endacott has upset you?"

"Indeed he has!" he answered at once. "He made insinuations concerning our meeting in Exeter which no man of honour could tolerate. When I demanded an apology, or that he should give me satisfaction in the manner which is usual in England . . ."

"Do you mean . . ."

"A duel, of course. I have been told they are common enough here, although illegal."

"Have you ever handled a sword?"

"No, but I dare swear I would have acquitted myself well enough."

He stood straight-backed, the cleft of his chin very pronounced, his dark eyes bold and confident.

"That was brave of you," Charlotte said warmly. "What was Mr. Endacott's reaction?"

"He apologised," John answered disgustedly. "Though not immediately, 'tis true. He said he had never considered a duel to be a reasonable way to settle an argument or misunderstanding, and invited me to explain why I travelled in his carriage with you. When I had done—and 'tis a wonder he made sense of what I said, I was so angry—he offered me a glass of madeira and asked my pardon."

"You sound as if that did not please you."

"I consider it a sign of weakness. Do you suppose *I* would have refused a challenge such as I offered him?"

"And yet, he was surely right? It would have settled nothing if either of you had been killed or injured."

"Are you taking his side, then?" John demanded.

"I was only suggesting that what to you seemed akin to cowardice, appears to me more like common sense."

John shrugged. "Naturally you would not understand, being a woman. I concede that Mr. Endacott had some justification for his suspicions. I am not a rich man, and though you are an orphan, you are nonetheless a member of one of the wealthiest families in this part of the country. What could be more tempting for a man quick to grasp opportunities? At least, that is how your guardian viewed the matter."

"No wonder you were so angry!" Charlotte exclaimed sympathetically. "And he provoked me in the same manner, accusing me of impropriety without waiting for an explanation. Did you discover how he knew you had travelled in his carriage?"

"Someone must have seen us, I suppose, and reported to him."

"If he listens to gossip, his conduct is all the more offensive."

Suddenly John laughed. "I' faith, he *has* riled you, Miss Charlotte. And I dare swear he thought himself the very paragon of a guardian, protecting his ward from a wily adventurer."

"You are assured he is my guardian?"

"Yes. He offered to procure a copy of the document he signed in Plymouth."

She said thoughtfully, "In that case, I surmise he has every right to order my future—even arrange a marriage for me."

"I suppose so. But you must not be anxious on that score, for . . ."

"I have every reason to be anxious," she broke in, "it seems I shall be given to the first suitor who can be bribed by the assurance of a generous dowry. Mr. Endacott informed me that his fiancée probably had the matter in hand already."

John stared at her in dismay. "Then, by heaven *you* have every reason to be angry!"

"And humiliated," she confessed. "I am no beauty, nor endowed with exceptional gifts. But, when I have been in England only a few days, for him to imply that I should have no chance . . ." She broke off, biting her lip.

John took hold of her hand. "Do not so belittle yourself. You may perhaps lack what a gentleman like Mr. Endacott finds most pleasing in a woman, but you have qualities *I* greatly admire. You have accepted hardship and responsibility without complaint or self-pity. You are courageous . . ."

"I had little courage left when I met you in Exeter."

"That is perfectly understandable. You must be confident that you can conquer all adversity, achieve any object you set yourself, and it will be so. That is how I have lived and how I intend to live." He freed her hand and pulled at his lower lip. "The question of your marriage, though, poses a difficulty for me. For if I seek your company, it will be concluded I am indeed the adventurer your guardian first took me for. Mr. Endacott made no mention of this dowry to me. But who will believe that?"

"I believe it," she said earnestly.

He smiled at her. "Then who else's opinion matters? Save that I would have it known I have no liking for bribery. When I choose a wife, it will be because she is the right woman to help me, not on account of any dowry she might have." He picked up his hat. "Now I must take my leave, for I have work to do." He glanced round the book-lined room, at the carved writing-table, the thick carpet and silver candelabra. "One day I shall have as fine a library as this. But in an American house, not an English one. Though I grant Stokeleigh is quite to my liking."

"I find it a little overwhelming," Charlotte admitted. "There are so many rooms and so much furniture. Compared with my previous life, this should seem paradise, and yet . . . Will you think me foolish if I say that I feel this is not a happy house?"

"What makes you say that?"

"Our house in Southport was small and sparsely furnished, yet everything in it was cherished. Here, it is as if every object has been valued for its worth alone, as if nothing has ever been touched with—with love. Now you *will* deem me fanciful."

John smiled at her indulgently. "Your feelings are more natural to a woman than a man, and your imagination heightened by your circumstances."

"Perhaps you are right. Mr. Endacott has spoken of the disputes in his—our family. Apart from quarrelling amongst themselves, they seem also to have aroused antipathy in the district."

"So I have learned, even in this short time. It seems the Endacotts have been hard task-masters, putting down by force any demand for higher wages or better conditions. There was even an occasion when the military were brought in to quell an uprising which began quite peaceably. Innocent people were injured and thrown into gaol. Men do not forget such things."

"Mr. Endacott declares he wishes to end such injustices, and to better the conditions of his workpeople."

"Then he had best make haste. For, judging by what I have heard, 'tis a wonder some member of the family has not been murdered before now. Why, there is even a tale of a Tiverton man having returned from transportation and vowing revenge upon the Endacotts who were responsible for sending him away. Oh, do not look so alarmed, Miss Charlotte. Men often talk in such fashion. But when it comes to the test, 'tis scarcely likely to happen. I should be surprised if a man who has survived twenty years of transportation would risk putting his neck in a gallow's noose."

Charlotte ate her supper alone, in the big dining-room. Gervase had gone out, his housekeeper told her, and given no indication of when he would return.

"And that's not like him," Mrs. Yeo declared. "In fact, I don't know what can be the matter with Mr. Gervase. You'd have thought he'd come back from Plymouth happy as a king, seeing he's the late Mr. Matthew's heir and can be as free with his money now as he likes. Instead, he seems properly put out. I hope he's not sickening for something. He was delicate as a child, though the mistress wouldn't hear of it. Treated him just as if he was as strong as those two great brothers of his. But never a word of complaint you'd get from Mr. Gervase. The quiet one of the family he's always been. Though, to be sure, he talks enough these days. Not that I can understand the half of what he says, 'tis above my head the way he uses words."

Charlotte, overawed by the size of Stokeleigh, had tried to picture it as a house wherein a family had been raised. But she could find no indication that children had ever lived there, save the portraits on the first landing. She had studied those portraits, for most of these people, she supposed, were related to her in some way. There was only one to which she felt drawn: a fair-haired beautiful woman with hazel eyes and a sweet smile. Charlotte had supposed her to be Gervase's mother, she so resembled him in features and colouring. Yet the gentleness of expression did not accord with what little she had learned of the late Mrs. Endacott.

Taking a lighted candle from a maidservant, she went up the wide staircase and across the landing to the passage leading to her bedroom. She did not like this passage. It was oak-panelled and dark. The window at the far end was over-shadowed by trees, and the doors were recessed. She had no liking for places where people could hide, as the Indians hid in the woods of Maine. Nervously she peered ahead, then caught her breath. Framed in the pale light of the unshuttered window was the figure of a man.

Charlotte was on the point of swift retreat when the man spoke, and she recognised Gervase's voice.

"I am sorry if I frightened you," he said, coming towards her. "You had best let me take the candle. Your hands do not appear to be too steady."

"I—I did not know you were in the house," she faltered, feeling embarrassed and foolish.

"I came in a short while ago, by the side door. You are going to bed?"

"Yes," she answered shortly.

He went before her along the passage, holding the candle high. As they neared the window, the flame flickered and he shielded it with his hand. She realised then that the window was open.

"I like to walk in the garden at night," he said. "The sound of the river is very restful. You can hear it faintly from that window. I was sitting there listening to it. It has started to rain, that is why I came in."

Charlotte wondered why he should consider it necessary to make such a full explanation. Opening the door of her bedroom, he stood aside, and handed her the candlestick.

"I expect you are tired, cousin Charlotte, too tired for us to talk tonight. In the morning, I shall hope to make my peace with you."

It seemed to her that he was deliberately trying to be rid of her presence.

"As you wish," she said coolly, and turned away.

She was about to shut the door when the dogs in the stable yard started to bark. Gervase hurried to the passage window.

"What has set them off?" Charlotte asked.

He shrugged. "A poacher, probably. We get quite a number, especially on overcast nights such as this. I will send Thomas out to see. Go to bed, cousin Charlotte, and do not have a moment's anxiety. No danger threatens *you,* I do assure you."

When he left her, Charlotte went into her room and set down the candle. Why had Gervase been at such pains to reassure her? She had not supposed she was in any danger. Why should she be? She had no enemies in England; nor in America for that matter. Then what he said that afternoon came to mind. "It is as well you should be warned of the reception you will be met with in Tiverton when you admit to the name of Endacott." And John had suggested it was a wonder no member of the family had been murdered before now.

Was that why Gervase had spoken so jerkily, seemed so on edge? Did he fancy there was some danger, not to her, but to himself? And in his own garden?

Thoughtfully she began to undress. Then, on impulse, she flung a dressing-wrapper about her shoulders, and leaving the candle behind, went quietly from the room and along the passage to where she could observe the staircase and the hall. By the light of the wall sconces she saw Gervase come out of the library and cross to a passage which gave, she had discovered, on to a little door leading into the garden. At its entrance he paused to examine something in his hands. Charlotte saw, to her dismay, that it was a pistol.

For a few moments after he disappeared she hesitated, then went swiftly back the way she had come, her fear of the dark passage overshadowed by anxiety as to what might be happening in the garden. She passed her bedroom door and went to the window. Keeping well back in the shadows, she peered down. Dimly she could make out the terrace and the low parapet covered with roses. Beyond were the lawn and formal beds, bisected by the path to the iron gate and the river. Faintly she could hear the sound of water. Nothing else, for the dogs had ceased their barking.

She waited a long time, with eyes and ears alert, by the open window. At length she went to bed, cold and stiff, no nearer discovering what had alarmed the dogs and caused Gervase to go armed into the garden. She lay wakeful, trying to convince herself that if there had in fact been an intruder, it was no more than a poacher as Gervase had said. But in that case, why had he been so evasive, why have thought it necessary to reassure her so insistently? And why had he not sent Thomas out, as he had told her he would?

She went to sleep at last, only to dream of being chased by Indians, of running and running until, breathless, she found herself in John's arms. And he was holding a pistol and saying, "You will marry Gervase Endacott or I will kill him, even if I am transported for life."

She woke from the confused dream, her heart thumping, her hands and neck clammy.

"Bella," she called instinctively, and stretched out an arm.

But no one answered and her groping fingers closed, not upon her old nurse's warm skin, but on the curtains of the high, four-poster bed. There was no comfort there. Nor in the shuttered darkness of the big bedroom so far from home. But she had no home, she reminded herself, turning restlessly on the soft mattress; neither in England nor in America. No *real* home, where she was welcome and wanted. And Bella would never again answer her call in the night.

IV

Charlotte was finishing her breakfast next morning when Gervase entered the dining-room. He poured himself a mug of ale and stood looking down at her.

"I surmise I am still in disfavour with you? And in truth I do not blame you. I was hasty and tactless. You spoke of my causing you hurt and humiliation. For that I am deeply sorry. There," he added, tipping up the mug, "if any man made a more handsome or sincere apology, I have yet to meet him. Am I forgiven, cousin Charlotte?"

Carefully she folded her napkin. "Yes, I suppose so."

"You do not sound too sure."

She rose and faced him. "You may be sure, at least, that I shall not test your skill with a sword, *or* a pistol."

A wariness showed in his eyes. He said guardedly, "I do not follow your meaning." Then his face cleared and he laughed. "Oh, I see. Your American friend has told you that he was all for calling me out? I' faith, at one point I thought he would positively force a duel upon me."

"And you were not prepared to fight him?"

He looked at her in surprise. "Certainly not, in the circumstances. I'll wager Mr. Standish is very handy with his clenched fist, for he held it most threateningly beneath my chin. But I doubt if he has any skill with the foils, which is the weapon I should naturally choose. Even if I had agreed to pistols, he would need to be an expert shot."

"Because you are so good a marksman?"

He poured himself more ale. "I manage tolerably well."

Riled by his superior manner, she asked bitingly, "Have you fought many duels?"

He paused with the mug half-way to his mouth. Then, to her surprise, he burst out laughing. "You ask the most extraordinary questions in a delightfully innocent way. No, I have not fought even one duel, nor do I intend to do so."

"Not in any circumstances?"

"Oh, I would not go so far as to say that. But duelling is both foolish and illegal, and rarely resorted to in this part of the country. You surely would not prefer me to fight Mr. Standish, and in all probability either kill or wound him, rather than ask him for an explanation which, in the event, proved me to be in the wrong?"

"Naturally not. But Mr. Standish, for his part, was quite certain he would have bested you."

"I can well believe that," Gervase said equably. "He is a most assured young man. I should not be surprised if he ended up as a governor of one of your colonies."

"That is most unlikely. He is opposed to the present form of government."

"Indeed? And do you share his views?"

"I do not understand politics," she admitted. "There is, I know, a good deal of unrest at what some people regard as the high-handed attitude of the English government, and Mr. Standish has promised to explain the facts to me."

Gervase put down the mug and wiped his mouth on a fine linen handkerchief. "You admire him, do you not?"

"Yes," she answered directly. "And I am grateful to him. He has been very kind to me."

"Which I have not?"

She flushed, and said quickly, "I was not implying that. You are so very different. I confess I find you puzzling."

"That is not to be wondered at," he said lightly. "There was only one person who ever understood me—my maternal grandmother. Come, I will show you her portrait."

Charlotte followed him from the dining-room and across the hall. At the entrance to the passage where she had seen him prime a pistol, she asked, "Did you catch the poacher last night?"

Abruptly he stopped and glanced back at her, the wary expression again in his eyes. But when he answered, his tone was as casual as hers.

"I am afraid not. Thomas could find no sign of anyone in the garden. It was probably a fox which set the dogs barking."

"You did not yourself go out to investigate?"

He raised his eyebrows. "It is not my concern to chase poachers or foxes."

Charlotte said no more. She was following him up the stairs when he gave her more cause for speculation. He had been mounting leisurely, a hand on the banister. But at the turn of the staircase he deliberately crossed to the inner side and trod on the painted woodwork instead of the carpet.

Charlotte asked impulsively, "Is there something wrong with those treads? Are they dangerous?"

Gervase stopped, but did not look round. Hs voice was strained as he answered her.

"No, there is nothing wrong with them, except . . . It is merely a whim on my part that I avoid those particular stairs. It dates from childhood, when I saw . . . But no, I shall not distress you with that story." He pointed upwards. "There, that is my grandmother."

He was indicating the portrait of the beautiful fair-haired woman.

"I had wondered if she was your mother," Charlotte said. "You are so like her."

His mouth tightened. He gestured towards another painting, hung in a darker part of the landing. "That is my mother," he said and his voice was cold.

The portrait was of a woman dressed in a dark gown of heavy material, her hair drawn severely back from an angular face. The eyes were expressionless, the mouth thin-lipped. It was difficult to realise that she must be the daughter of the sweet-faced woman Charlotte had admired.

When she made no comment, Gervase continued to identify. "That is my father. When you have seen him, you have seen all the Endacotts."

She could appreciate his meaning. For already she had noticed the resemblance to her own father, though this man, short-necked and thickset, showed none of her father's kindness and humour.

"These are my brothers," Gervase continued, moving on. "Henry, the proper heir to Stokeleigh. And Stephen, two years younger, who died at the same time as Henry."

She would have liked to question him but decided against it. Instead, she remarked, "There does not appear to be a portrait of yourself. Do you not like being painted?"

He flicked the lace at his cuff. "I made a vow that I would not sit for a portrait until there was some good reason for my being remembered. That time has not yet come." He gave her a wry smile. "You will think me full of whims, cousin Charlotte."

"I have already told you, I find you puzzling," she said. Then recklessly she burst out, "For one thing, you do not always tell the truth."

He laughed. "That is a failing which can be laid at most people's doors, surely? In what particular instance have I defaulted in your estimation?"

"You told me it was not your concern to go after poachers. But I saw you, last night. I saw you cross the hall and go along the passage which leads to the garden. You had a pistol in your hand."

They were standing by the big window overlooking the drive. Clearly she saw a shadow cross his face, and he would not meet her eyes.

"I would rather you had not witnessed that," he said. "And I would ask you not to mention it to anyone. I am not very proud of my behaviour last night. I acted against my better judgment, against my resolve to have no more bloodshed laid at . . ." He raised his head, listening. "We have a visitor, I think."

Charlotte looked out of the window. She could hear horses, but the trees hid the riders from view. Then she caught a glimpse of red between the branches.

"Why, it is Sophia!" Gervase exclaimed. "Doubtless she has come to make your acquaintance. Come, we will go down to greet her."

Hastily Charlotte patted her hair and smoothed the collar of her blue woollen gown.

"Do not be frightened of meeting Sophia," Gervase said. "Her three sisters are all younger than she is and she has had the care of them for many years. It is possible she may attempt to order your life as she does theirs, but . . ."

"I thought that was exactly what you wished. You told me that Miss Pendleton would already be seeking a husband for me."

Gervase rubbed his cheek. "Oh, as to that, the matter is not urgent."

"It seemed so, yesterday," she reminded him. "What has made you change your mind? The visit of Mr. Standish?"

"He certainly holds you in high regard. If you should develop a liking for him . . ."

"You would raise no objection?"

"It is too soon to say that, too early to judge."

"Would it help your judgment if I told you that Mr. Standish is not in the least interested in the dowry you

57

mentioned? In fact, should you offer one, he would refuse."

His reaction was not what she expected.

"I think I hurt you yesterday more than I realised," he said sadly. "And I believe you will never forgive me for that."

He turned and crossed the landing. At the bend of the stairs, he made again for the wall. Then deliberately, he gripped the banister and trod firmly on the centre of the stairs which previously he had avoided. He looked up at her with a twisted smile.

"It seems you have the power to lay ghosts, cousin Charlotte. Come now and show yourself to Sophia."

In some trepidation, Charlotte went with him on to the terrace. Two horses stood beside the mounting-block. A groom was assisting a woman to dismount, a woman in a crimson velvet riding suit. As Sophia Pendleton came towards them, Charlotte saw that she was extraordinarily handsome, with thick dark hair and a high colour. She wore a stylish black hat with a trailing ostrich feather and carried a silver-handled whip. The gravel crunched under her boots.

It seemed to Charlotte that if Gervase's fiancée had been a duchess she could not have been more impressive, and her immediate reaction was to make her lowest curtsey. Instead, she nerved herself to take the leather-gloved hand outstretched in greeting.

"So this is your little cousin from America, Gervase," Sophia said in a condescending tone. "I hope you are treating her kindly."

"Mr. Endacott has been most thoughtful for my welfare," Charlotte said before Gervase could reply.

She saw the quizzical lift of his eyebrows. Sophia's bold gaze moved over Charlotte from head to toe.

"I was not prepared for so pretty a child, Gervase. You did her less than justice by your description."

"She—she has changed," he said awkwardly, "since our first meeting. At that time . . ."

"I was suffering from the effects of a long and distressing voyage," Charlotte broke in, and saw the surprise on Sophia's face.

"It seems Miss Endacott is well able to speak up for herself. That again I was not prepared for. Indeed, Gervase, I should have known better than to trust your judgment."

Hastily he suggested that they should take a turn on the lawn. " 'Tis too fine a morning to spend indoors."

"Very well," Sophia agreed, tucking a hand beneath his arm in a proprietary manner. "But, as you know, I like my chocolate promptly at twelve o'clock."

"Mrs. Yeo will doubtless attend to it," he said resignedly. "And she will provde ale for your groom, though he is not in favour with me at present."

"Why not?"

"Because of his gossiping tongue." Gervase offered his other arm to Charlotte, who rested her fingers lightly on his sleeve. "The gentleman he saw driving in my carriage was an American friend of Charlotte's. He came over on the same ship and they met again by chance in Exeter."

"What a delightful coincidence," Sophia remarked in a tone of the utmost disbelief. "Miss Endacott should be warned, however, that such chance meetings and impulsive invitations for gentlemen to drive with her, can give rise to malicious gossip."

Charlotte saw the tightening of Gervase's mouth. He said coldly, "Before you criticise my cousin, Sophia, it would be as well to . . ." He broke off, silenced by the look Sophia gave him. He said lamely, "The roses are very fine this year, are they not?"

Charlotte's annoyance changed to amusement. It occurred to her that they must look a strange trio, pacing so solemnly across the grass, with Gervase patently intent on trying to please both women.

"Tell me," Sophia was saying, "have you broached the subject of a maid to your ward?"

"Not yet," he admitted reluctantly.

"Or the matter of a suitable wardrobe?"

"No, not that, either. I have had other, more pressing matters, on my mind. But, Sophia, there is not the slightest reason why you should not discuss these matters with Charlotte. I am sure she will be only too willing to accept your help."

Hopefully he glanced at Charlotte. Still amused, she said at once, "Of course, ma'am. I shall be most grateful for your advice on the matter of clothes."

Sophia looked gratified. "I have an excellent dressmaker in Tiverton who would be delighted to make you some new gowns. Though, to be sure," she added patronisingly, "the one you are wearing is in very good taste, if, perhaps, a trifle *démodé.*"

"I dare say it is at least two years out of date," Charlotte agreed blandly. "In the colonies we suffer the disadvantage of distance when trying to follow the current fashion."

Gervase attempted to withdraw. "If you two ladies are about to discuss fashion . . ."

Sophia held tightly to his arm. "No, we will do that at the dressmaker's. There is this other matter, of Miss Endacott's future . . ."

"I am sure that can be arranged most satisfactorily," Gervase broke in hastily.

"Indeed? That, again is not what you gave me to understand yesterday. You were only too willing then that *I* should try to arrange . . ." She stopped, frowning, as Thomas came running from the little gate which gave on to the river path.

His wig was awry, his white breeches stained with mud, his shoes and stockings dripping water. At sight of the little group he came to a halt, breathing hard.

"Whatever is the matter?" Gervase demanded, releasing himself from his two companions. "Why are you in such a disgraceful state?"

"Oh, sir, 'tis . . ." The young footman passed a hand

across his forehead, leaving a filthy streak. "Give me a proper shock, it did."

"What gave you a shock?"

Thomas righted his wig and tried to wipe the mud from his breeches, but only made matters worse.

Sophia stepped forward. "Your master asked you a question. Answer him immediately."

Thomas looked stubborn. " 'Tis a matter for the master's ears alone, ma'am, not fit for ladies."

"Do not be absurd! I have not been reared in a nunnery. Neither, I surmise, has Miss Endacott. Have you been in a brawl?"

Thomas shook his head and glanced appealingly at Gervase. "There's been an accident, sir. It don't make pretty hearing."

"Then you will say no more about it," Gervase said quietly. "Not until these ladies have gone indoors."

Obediently Charlotte turned and began to walk towards the house. She heard Sophia's voice, raised in protest. And then Gervase's, quietly insistent.

"I pray you will do as I say, Sophia. If there has been an accident, help is needed. Your presence can only be a hindrance."

Charlotte looked over her shoulder. Sophia drew herself up, her fingers tightening on her whip. With long strides, the skirt of her crimson habit trailing on the grass, she went across the garden and on to the terrace. Without waiting for her groom, she mounted her black mare and galloped recklessly down the drive.

It was an hour later, and Charlotte was browsing through the books in the library, when Gervase appeared. He looked pale and strained. He perched on the edge of the writing-table and aimlessly moved a paper-knife to and fro.

"As Thomas was at pains to tell me," he said heavily, "it was no sight for ladies."

"If you would prefer not to tell me . . ," Charlotte suggested.

"You will hear soon enough, even if I keep silent. And doubtless the tale will not lose in the telling once it starts being bruited around the district. The plain facts are that some unfortunate fellow, a man not known in the village, apparently fell from the bridge, into the river, and Thomas discovered him when he went to inspect the fish-traps."

"You mean he was drowned? Oh, how dreadful!"

"It is not clear whether he died from drowning or from an injury to his head. And yet it seems unlikely that he was set upon, for there would appear to be no motive. He was obviously a labourer, very poorly clothed."

"When did this happen?"

"Presumably last night," Gervase answered and dug the point of the paper-knife into the tooled leather of the desk.

Last night. The words repeated themselves in Charlotte's mind. Last night the dogs had barked and Gervase had gone into the garden with a pistol in his hand. He had lied about his movements until she challenged him, and then he had said . . . What was it he had said? "I would rather you had not witnessed that . . . I ask you not to repeat it . . . I am not proud of my behaviour last night." And he had spoken of bloodshed, she could not remember the exact words.

She looked at him as he sat on the desk, swinging his leg, and fiddling with the paper-knife, so obviously ill-at-ease.

She asked, "If this man was not attacked, how do you account for the injury to his head?"

"There is a simple explanation, though whether the constable I have sent for will accept it . . . The river is low at present, leaving the stones by the weir almost uncovered. Probably the poor fellow hit his head as he fell. Though why he should lean over the parapet at night, unless he was drunk, is difficult to understand."

"And you do not know who he is?"

"Not yet."

"Perhaps," she said, watching him intently, "he was the intruder you suspected of being in your garden."

Gervase threw aside the paper-knife and stood up. "Yes," he said and his voice sounded weary. "That is exactly what I fear."

A little shiver went down Charlotte's back and her hands felt cold. Why should he use the word "fear"? Of what was he afraid? That he had killed a man and would be discovered? He had lied to her, and told her to keep quiet about his actions. Was he then expecting her to be asked questions? When the constable came, would he ask to see her and, if so, what should she tell him? That she had heard that Gervase's life was threatened; that he had gone armed into the garden on suspicion of an intruder, and then denied doing so and later admitted that he was ashamed of whatever he had done last night?

Gervase went across to the window and stood with his back to her, hands clasped beneath his coat. His voice still had the same note of weariness.

"That makes the fifth life in ten years that stretch of the river has claimed. A cottager's child, a young woman who threw herself over the bridge when deserted by her love; this poor fellow and—my brothers."

"Your brothers?" she echoed in surprise.

"Have you not been told? In that case my servants, especially Thomas, must have been unusually reticent. It was an accident, a foolish waste of lives. Henry challenged Stephen—they were always laying wagers and trying to best each other, at horse racing or tree climbing or shooting. This time the bet was that Stephen could not go over the weir in flood and stay dryer than Henry. They had done it before and so had I, in small boats, when we were boys. But they were grown men and should have been beyond such escapades. The river was running especially fast after a storm in the hills. But they might have succeeded, if they had not quarrelled."

"What happened?" Charlotte asked as he paused.

"They argued about their positions at starting. Henry was about to step into his boat when Stephen struck him. Henry staggered and clutched at Stephen. They fell into the deep water above the weir. They were both wearing greatcoats and heavy boots. They were swept over the weir in a matter of seconds."

"You saw it happen?"

He sighed heavily. "Yes, from the bridge. The men were all out in the fields, the women at their cooking. The only person in sight was old Matt the shepherd. It was he who hauled them out, with his crook."

"And you could do nothing to save them?"

He shook his head. "Nothing. If you had ever seen this river in spate, you would realise that. They must have been a quarter of a mile downstream before I could even reach the bank. All *I* could do was to inform my parents. I think they never forgave me."

"Surely they could not blame you for what happened?"

"No, not for that. Matt bore out my story and, in any case, everyone knew how reckless my brothers were. But I think my parents never forgave me for being alive when Henry and Stephen were dead. Sophia felt the same way, too. She was betrothed to Henry, you see."

At Charlotte's exclamation, he turned. "That surprises you? I have already told you that marriages in this country are, for the most part, arranged. It so happened that Henry's and Sophia's wishes ran hand-in-hand with my father's. As far as Sophia is concerned, I am a poor second-best. As far as I am concerned, in this as in all else, I had no choice." He came across the room and stood looking down at Charlotte. "Tell me, what did you think of Sophia?"

Taken by surprise, Charlotte replied guardedly, "She is a very handsome woman."

"And a determined one? 'Tis natural she should be. She was left in charge, when quite young, of a big house and three younger sisters. Her father is frequently ailing, and the youngest girl, Becky, suffers from a weak chest. Do not judge Sophia too hastily on this morning's episode. She will be back soon enough, I'll wager, if only out of curiosity about the accident."

V

Gervase was wrong. Sophia did not come back, either that day or the next morning.

"If she chooses to be piqued," Gervase said, "we will manage without her. I will escort you into Tiverton, and you may go to the dressmaker my mother employed and order what you need."

"But I have no money," Charlotte reminded him. "Or am I to suppose that Great-uncle Matthew made provision for me?"

"His will was made before he was even aware of your existence," Gervase told her. "But I am sure he would have wished me to provide for all your needs. You must have no qualms on that score."

"If I might purchase some material, I am well able to make my own clothes."

Gervase laughed. "You would cause Mrs. Yeo to have the vapours if she came upon you doing so. No, Charlotte, if you are so anxious to occupy your hands, we will buy a piece of embroidery or tapestry."

"And what will I do with it when it is completed?" she asked. "For, indeed, your house seems overfull of knick-knacks already."

He raised his eyebrows. "Are you not planning to have a home of your own one day?"

"If I were to employ my fingers to that end," she said

sharply, "it would not be on such fripperies as a piece of embroidery."

Gervase sighed and helplessly shook his head. "You had best please yourself, then, as to what you can purchase. Go and put on your riding suit and then . . ." He glanced at her anxiously. "I suppose you *can* ride?"

"Of course I can," she answered impatiently. "My father had a pony, though naturally it did not compare with anything in your stables. You need not fear that I shall fall off within the first few minutes."

"Even so," he said doubtfully, "I think the grey mare will suit you best. She is quiet and easy to manage."

Riled, Charlotte said, "It is clear that you have a poor opinion of my capabilities."

"On the contrary, I am now realising how wrong was my first impression. I am beginning to think that acting as your guardian will present me with even greater problems than I anticipated."

"Then I will do my best to banish them as soon as possible," she retorted. "Though I cannot conceive that, even to be rid of me, you would have me throw myself at Mr. Standish's head."

She was gratified to see that once again she had disconcerted Gervase. He rubbed his cheek.

"I am at a loss to understand how I can provoke you so easily, cousin Charlotte, when it is not my intention to do so."

"I dare say the fault is in myself," Charlotte said, colouring. "But I do not relish the idea of being beholden to someone who regards me as a problem and a burden."

"Charlotte, I . . ." Gervase stretched out his hand. Then, as she remained coldly silent, he gave up. Shrugging, he turned towards the door. "I will go and tell Benedict to saddle the mare."

Charlotte went up to her bedroom, annoyed both with Gervase and herself. "Put on your riding suit," he had said, taking it for granted that she had one.

If he expected her to appear in a crimson velvet habit
and a wide-brimmed hat with a sweeping ostrich feather,
like Sophia, he would be disappointed. The only dress
she had that was suitable for riding was of dark blue
wool, buttoned down the front, with long tight sleeves
and white collar and cuffs; and a high-crowned hat made
of beaver skin. Aunt Lucy, upon first seeing this en-
semble, had declared it made Charlotte look like a Puritan. It had been perfectly suitable for Southport, even
in Salem. But here . . . Here it would perfectly match
a quiet grey mare and her own status as Gervase's ward.

Irritably Charlotte pulled open a drawer to find her
gloves. Lying on a shawl was the doll Gervase had
given her. She picked it up and clumsily manipulated
the strings, making the puppet's limbs jerk in all directions. Gervase had bought it for the little girl he supposed her to be. And, it seemed to Charlotte, that girl
still existed in his mind. Or, if he *had* accepted the fact
that his ward was a young woman of nineteen, the picture of a simple, tractable child was infinitely to be
preferred, so that he chose to see the illusion rather than
the reality.

But she was not a child, and she had shouldered too
many responsibilities and become too independent to be
treated in such a superior fashion by a man only six
years older than herself.

Tossing the doll on to a chair, she changed into the
dark blue dress. Then, about to leave her bedroom, she
glanced back. The puppet lay sprawled on the chair, its
gaily coloured skirt crumpled, its dark eyes staring re-
proachfully at her. Sighing, she picked it up, smoothing the bright dress, straightening the twisted limbs.
Carefully she laid it on the shawl and shut the drawer.
After all, she told herself, the gift had been well meant.
If she had indeed been the child Gervase expected,
could any man have chosen a more charming toy to
make a little girl feel welcome? It was no more his fault

than hers that they had both started their odd relationship with a misconception.

He was waiting for her beside the mounting-block. He wore buckskin breeches and a green broadcloth coat with brass buttons on the wide cuffs. The ribbon which tied his hair matched his brown tricorne. Charlotte could not imagine him ever looking anything but elegant.

She wondered if he would remark on her lack of proper riding habit, but his comment surprised her.

"When Sophia sees your hat," he said, assisting her to mount, "she will doubtless wish to have it copied at once. Though such a style would not suit her as well as it does you."

She looked at him, suspecting sarcasm. But his expression was ingenuous, and his smile had none of the falseness she had seen in Plymouth.

The grey mare was not what she expected. Instead of a solid, broad-backed creature, it was a slender-legged thoroughbred, which turned its head with gentle inquisitiveness as Charlotte put her foot in the stirrup. Once in the saddle, she felt very high up. Remembering her over-confident words to Gervase, she was relieved he had assured her the mare was easy to manage, for it would be a long way to fall.

While Gervase adjusted her stirrup leather, she said, "I have been wondering about the doll."

He glanced up at her, puzzled. "The doll?"

"The one you gave me on board the ship. I still have it. Would you like me to give it back to you?"

He bent his head as he pulled at the strap. "Keep it, Charlotte. Keep it to give to your firstborn daughter."

Then, as if the thought naturally followed, he said, "Doubtless while we are in Tiverton, you would wish to visit Mr. Standish?"

"He will be working, at the school. Blundell's, I think it is called."

"Then we will go there and see how he is progressing. Is he a good architect?"

"I have no idea. But surely he must be or this merchant in Boston would not have sent him over here, paying all his expenses for as long as he thinks it necessary to stay."

"He is not tied to a set time?" Gervase asked, mounting and starting off down the drive.

"Apparently not. He has to visit certain cities and observe different types of architecture, but I think Mr. Roberts places great confidence in him."

Gervase said thoughtfully, "Then I have a mind to ask him to draw me up some plans for the new cottages I intend building to replace those near the river."

"Are there not local men who would do that?"

"Naturally. But I am in favour of encouraging a young man with ideas and ambitions."

Charlotte's first reaction was to be gratified by such a proposal. Then another thought struck her. Was not Gervase's real reason for wishing to employ John more subtle? Was it not a way of providing the younger man with sufficient money to marry, since John had declared he would not accept any dowry offered him on her behalf? It was merely another idea, she thought bitterly, that Gervase had thought up, the sooner to be rid of her.

As they rode through the village, she became aware of the latent hostility amongst the cottagers. The women gossiping in their doorways stopped and stared. They bobbed curtsies, bidding their children do the same. But there was no real deference in their actions and their faces bore a wary, closed look.

The river, as Gervase had said, was low. It flowed placidly between the solid stone arches of the bridge, rippled along the bed of pebbles, then cascaded gently over the weir. It was difficult to believe that this tranquil stretch of water had claimed so many lives, or could constitute a threat to the row of cottages which had been built, a little apart from the rest of the village, upon the river bank.

Gervase pointed with his whip. "You can see how easily a man could fall over the bridge, head first on to the stones."

She saw that what he said was true. If a man were drunk, as Gervase had suggested, he could easily topple over the low parapet.

She said thoughtfully, "But if that was what happened, would he not have been found lying on the pebbles, for the water is very shallow there?"

Gervase rubbed his cheek. "That was what puzzled the constable. My guess is that poor Biddlecombe was knocked unconscious by the fall. Then, when the water revived him, he tried to reach the bank, but fell into the deeper channel on the farther side which carried him over the weir. I have traced the course with a heavy branch, and it is feasible."

But was it a true explanation? Or one he had ingeniously thought up? Recalling his evasive manner, and the words which had so aroused her suspicions, Charlotte could not decide.

She said, "You mentioned a name. You have now discovered the identity of the man?"

Gervase's face took on again the closed, wary look. "Yes," he said shortly. "He was a Tiverton man, lately returned from overseas." Then, before she could ask any more questions, he urged his horse forward. "Let us ride on, cousin Charlotte. There is not the slightest need for you to trouble your head any further about this unfortunate matter."

Again, she suspected there was a warning in his words. Yet it seemed to her incredible that this elegant, quiet-voiced young man could be guilty of such a brutal crime as murdering a defenceless labourer and throwing his body into the river. But had the man been defenceless? From overseas, Gervase had said. Could that mean, from transportation? And had he indeed been the man who, according to John, had openly threatened to take Gervase's life?

Deliberately, as they rode on, Charlotte put the matter from her mind. It was a beautiful June morning. She felt well again after the ordeal of the Atlantic crossing. She was mounted on a fine mare and riding towards the man who, if all went well, would eventually take her back to her homeland. Gervase Endacott and his feuds were no concern of hers.

It was a pleasant ride along the turnpike road above the river. Gervase, who seemed bent on being an entertaining companion, kept up a lively description of the houses and farms along their route.

He pointed out a square, solid mansion, backed by a clump of elm trees, standing close beside the river.

"My nearest neighbour, Sir William Ransom, lives there. He is a man much given to sport, and never happier than when following a pack of hounds."

"Did you not mention his name in connection with the danger to the cottages if the river floods?"

"Yes. He intends to create some fishponds, and for that purpose he proposes to construct a dam. It is my fear that, should he do so, and the dam not hold, in time of severe flooding the water would come down in one great wave and engulf the six cottages you noticed were very close to the river."

"He does not agree with you?"

Gervase shook his head. "We rarely agree on anything. He is a good enough fellow in his way, but all body and little brain."

He drew her attention to a cottage where lived a reputed witch, then a sixteenth century manor house supposed to be haunted by a murdered Cavalier. To Charlotte, an awareness of the past was a new experience. In Maine, everyone was so concerned with the needs of day-to-day living and with plans for the future, that there was no time to dwell on what had gone before. In England, she realised, everything she saw was the outcome of what men had done in the past.

Whether they had ploughed the land or hewed wood or fought battles, the result was here before her eyes.

"You can see Tiverton now," Gervase was saying. "Those buildings down by the river are fulling mills. I will not weary you with describing all the processes of woollen manufacture, but almost every person in the town is connected with the trade. It has brought great prosperity to Devon, but unfortunately it is past its peak here."

As they entered the town, his manner changed. He rode in silence, bidding Charlotte keep close to him. Again she noticed the covert glances directed at them both, the lack of any warmth in the eyes of the men and women who acknowledged Gervase's greeting. They rode up a hill and across a bridge, passing some fine houses which Gervase, in answer to Charlotte's questions, told her belonged to woollen merchants.

"There were many more," he said, "but we have suffered two great fires which destroyed much of the town. Over there on the left is St. Peter's Church, and this is Fore Street which will take us down to Blundell's School. I have no doubt you are anxious to see Mr. Standish before you start your shopping."

If it had not been for the attitude of the townspeople, Charlotte would have enjoyed the ride through the town. The solid stone and brick houses seemed strange to her after the wooden ones of home. Despite Gervase's talk of poverty, she could see no evidence of it.

"We do not parade that side of life," he told her. "If you ventured behind the façades of the rich you would find very different conditions. Yet in Tiverton the poor have been fortunate. You will find records here of benefactions dating back hundreds of years." His mouth tightened. "But not one bears the name of Endacott."

They crossed another bridge, spanning the Loman river, and bore right-handed.

"We are almost there," Gervase said. "It was a fine concept for a man who started as a poor boy carrying out errands for the kersey makers to wish to create a place of learning. It was unfortunate Peter Blundell did not live to see it completed."

"Mr. Standish considers the school small and old-fashioned."

Gervase frowned. " 'Tis none the worse for that. The Pendletons' manor dates back to 1560 but I think it one of the most attractive buildings I have ever seen. To Sophia, of course, it is nothing but an inconvenience. The management of Stokeleigh will be a deal more to her taste."

"When will you be married?"

Gervase shrugged. "Next year, perhaps."

Although he had explained that his marriage was entirely a matter arranged between two families, Charlotte was shocked by the indifference in his voice. In America, it had seemed to her, men and women married for love. Men chose their wives for their ability to withstand hardship and danger, to rear children in the most difficult circumstances and to succour their families in illness and misfortune; and, having chosen, gave and received loyalty and affection, if not always a deep passion. Gervase's cold, detached attitude towards his marriage was beyond her comprehension.

When they reached the school, he dismounted beside the porter's lodge and helped Charlotte down. She looked through the iron gates and saw, beyond a walled courtyard, a long low building with two porches. Then she caught sight of John. He was sitting on a patch of grass, bareheaded, a drawing-board on his knees. At the sound of their approach he glanced round, then sprang to his feet and came forward, hand outstretched.

"Miss Charlotte, what an unexpected pleasure!" He bowed formally to Gervase. "Your servant, sir."

Gervase raised his tricorne. "My cousin wished to make some purchases in the town and we thought it a good opportunity to inspect your work, with your permission."

"I shall be pleased for you to do so, though this is mere copying of another man's work."

He fetched his drawing-board and Gervase studied it closely.

"You appear to be a meticulous draughtsman," he remarked approvingly. "Charlotte tells me you are anxious to put your own ideas into practice."

"I want to build for the future, not the past. This place no doubt has served its purpose, but from the drawings I have seen of the College of William and Mary in Williamsburgh, it would make Blundell's School seem little more than a collection of cottages strung together. Oh, I know you will talk to me of traditon, but I believe we must make our own tradition in the colonies, and it must be an American one, not English."

"You speak almost as if you were of a different race," Gervase commented.

"There are people who appear to regard us as that," John said bitterly. "If there is a rift between England and the American colonies, your Government will have much to answer for. We want to be English, we want to be loyal to the crown, but men like Lord North are making it increasingly difficult. There is a limit to what we will endure at the hands of a Parliament three thousand miles distant." He smiled suddenly. "But let us not become involved in politics on so fine a morning. Will you do me the favour of taking some refreshments in my lodgings? My landlady is an excellent cook, her sweetmeats are to be recommended."

Charlotte glanced enquiringly at Gervase.

"Thank you, Mr. Standish," he said amiably. "We should be pleased to come."

John gathered up his drawing materials and put on his hat. "I have no horse with me but it is no distance to St. Andrew's Street where I lodge. I will go ahead of you and prepare Mrs. Bridle for your coming."

As they walked towards the gates, Gervase said, "I would like to see more of your work, Mr. Standish. It is possible that I could put a commission in your way."

John looked wary. "I am not sure that my ideas would please you, sir. They are probably too modern."

"In this case, that is what I require. I intend to replace some cottages and I do not wish the new buildings to be patterned on the present ones, which are too small and dark. If the idea interest you . . ."

"Certainly it does," John said eagerly. "I will have some drawings ready for you to see, at my lodgings, that you may judge how practical my ideas are."

"Mr. Standish is certainly a young man who has no doubt of his own abilities," Gervase observed as he and Charlotte mounted their horses, to follow leisurely in John's wake.

They had crossed the bridge over the Loman and were walking their mounts up Gold Street when Gervase broke off abruptly in mid-sentence.

"What is the matter?" Charlotte asked. "You look worried."

He did not answer at once, but following his gaze she saw ahead of them a group of men emerging from a doorway. They were shouting and guffawing, some staggering into the roadway. Charlotte caught sight of John, pushing his way through them.

"It appears there has been a rowdy meeting at the woolcombers' club," Gervase said. "Let us get past them quickly, Charlotte. They are good enough fellows on the whole, but when in liquor are somewhat unpredictable."

She heard the note of urgency in his voice. He reined back his horse, then moved forward on her near side. Tightening her grip on the reins, she urged the mare to the further side of the road. One of the men recognised Gervase. He had a tankard in his hand.

Waving it towards Gervase, he shouted. "There be the man as should pay for Kit Biddlecombe's burial."

There was an angry murmur from his companions. From somewhere out of sight a woman's voice repeated harshly, "Aye, he should pay, not the parish."

Charlotte glanced at Gervase. He had gone very pale, his mouth was set. The man with the tankard lurched forward.

"You killed Kit Biddlecombe, didn't 'ee, *Mister* Endacott? Kit come for 'ee night afore last, and no blame to un for that. But you got un first, didn't 'ee?"

"You're talking nonsense," Gervase said quietly. "Kit Biddlecombe died by falling over the bridge into the river."

The man drained his tankard, then tossed it over his shoulder. Wiping his mouth with the back of his hand, he came up to Gervase.

"What Kit didn't have a chance to do, I'll do for un. I'm his uncle, Sam's brother. Had you forgotten that? And two of our family dead at the 'ands of yourn be too much for me to stomach. Get down off that horse."

Gervase turned to Charlotte. "Ride on. Turn left beyond the Market Cross. Tell Mr. Standish to take you back to Stokeleigh."

As she hesitated, a man reeled across the road and laid a grimy hand on her skirt. Leaning across, Gervase brought his whip sharply down on the man's arm.

"Do as I say, Charlotte," he ordered. "This is no place for you."

He used his whip again, this time on the grey mare's flank. The animal bounded forward, so that Charlotte had to cling to the saddle. Rounding the corner, she came face to face with John, hastening back along the street.

"What has happened?" he demanded. "Where is Mr. Endacott?"

"Oh, John, I am frightened," she gasped. "They are threatening him."

"Who is threatening him?"

"Some men back there, woolcombers I think he called them. Half of them are drunk, and one spoke of—of killing Gervase."

"That is nonsense! Wait here while I go back and see what is happening."

"I shall come too."

He started to protest, but she had already turned the mare. John grasped her reins and led the animal. People ran past them, drawn by the commotion. Windows banged open, dogs set up a continuous barking. A youth had hold of Gervase's horse, but he was no longer in the saddle.

John looked up at Charlotte. His face was grim; his eyes betrayed his anxiety.

"There has been a lot of talk against Endacott, but I never thought . . . Charlotte, wait here."

As the crowd milled around her, she saw clenched fists raised, a club brandished. She saw the anxious faces of women at upstairs windows, and shopkeepers fearful of damage to their wares. Two well-dressed men, laying about them with their whips and calling for order, tried to force their horses through the shouting, swearing mob. Charlotte caught a momentary glimpse of Gervase, lying in the road amidst a welter of arms and legs and sticks. John had almost reached him when he called out.

"Get back, Standish. Stay with Charlotte."

As John hesitated, Gervase called again. "Do as I say, damn you. Get Charlotte away."

John fought his way out of the crowd and reached Charlotte's side.

"You heard what he said?"

She was suddenly aware of the curious stares directed at her, of fingers pointing, and harsh voices.

"It bain't Mistress Pendleton. Never seen 'er afore. She'm a 'foreigner.' " Then a woman's voice, louder than the rest. "I know who she be. She's an Endacott, the one from America."

The name was taken up on all sides. John's voice was tense.

"A few more yards and we shall reach my lodgings."

A dog ran into the road, snapping at the mare's heels. As the mare kicked out, its hoof caught an old woman with a basket of bread. She fell heavily, loaves spilling all around her.

Charlotte cried out in dismay, and would have stopped.

Then she saw the faces of the men and women who were surging towards her. Contorted with rage, they were more frightening than the face of any Indian she had ever seen.

"John, quickly," she gasped.

He lifted her from the saddle and ran with her to a house standing back from the road. With his elbow he raised the latch. The door gave at once. He almost fell inside, kicking it to behind them. As he set Charlotte on her feet, she fell against him. John's breath came hard, and he gripped her arms.

"It is all right now," he assured her. "They will not . . ."

A hammering on the door behind him cut short his words.

"There is a back door, giving on to a yard. From there we can reach the stables. I have a horse there."

Half-dragging Charlotte, he led the way through the house and into a small cobbled yard. Breathless, she leaned against the wall of the stable.

"They would not really attack me, surely?" she asked incredulously. "I have done them no harm."

Lifting down a saddle, John answered grimly. "You saw what mood they are in. It was enough that you bear the name of a family much hated in this town. But when your mare kicked the old woman . . ."

"I could not help that," she protested.

"Neither, if what you tell me is true, can your cousin be blamed for the misery his forbears caused. But he is the obvious scapegoat. And now, with the death of this returned convict . . ."

"Do *you* think Gervase killed him?"

John answered over his shoulder as he tightened the

girth. "How should I know? The fellow came back from transportation vowing vengeance on Gervase's father. When he discovered the old man was dead, he swore to avenge himself on your cousin instead."

Charlotte put her hands to her face. "It is all so horrible! And Gervase abhors violence of any kind."

John dragged the bridle over the horse's head. "So a man might declare in ordinary circumstances. But if his life is threatened, 'tis likely to be a different tale." He led out the animal. "I will mount first and lift you up. There is a lane nearby which will bring us eventually on the road to Stokeleigh."

They could still hear the uproar in the streets.

"It seems dreadful to leave Gervase," Charlotte said unhappily.

"It was his own wish," John pointed out.

"You sound—almost indifferent."

He reached down to lift her to the saddle. "I did my best to aid him, as you saw. My concern now is for your safety, not his. And Tiverton quarrels are not ours." He put his arm about her. "The sooner I have you safely at Stokeleigh, the better."

VI

Charlotte felt she could no longer keep silent about what had occurred on the night of Kit Biddlecombe's death. On the ride back to Stokeleigh, she told John of her suspicions and Gervase's theory of how the returned convict had died.

John was silent for a few minutes, then he said thoughtfully, "Surely if you sat at an open window, you could not have failed to hear the sound of a shot, had there been one?"

"I had not thought of that," she confessed, then recalled that nothing had been said about this man being shot, only that he had a head injury. "Gervase could have used the butt of the pistol, I suppose." As she realised what she was implying, she shook her head and said emphatically, "No, I cannot believe that. I am sure his explanation must be the true one, that the man fell over the parapet of the bridge."

John exclaimed impatiently, "Then let us leave it at that. As I have already told you, it is none of our affair."

But it was *her* affair. At least, what happened to Gervase in consequence of that night, concerned her deeply. For if he should be killed, what then would be her future? She would be more than ever alone, save for John. But she could scarcely expect John to make himself responsible for her when she was neither related nor betrothed to him.

In the midst of these anxious thoughts about her own future, she had a sudden recollection of Gervase, lying in the road amidst flailing fists and sticks, calling out to John to get her to safety; and she felt ashamed.

When they reached Stokeleigh, she immediately told Mrs. Yeo what had happened. The housekeeper sent for Tom and Benedict, who galloped off to Tiverton at once.

"I shall not leave until Mr. Endacott returns, or we have news of him," John declared.

They waited in the drawing-room, where one window overlooked the drive. The thought occurred to Charlotte that, should Gervase be killed, Sophia Pendleton would have to be told. Then again, impatiently, she took herself to task. It was unthinkable that Gervase should be killed—by a crowd of wool workers, in the middle of an English town in broad daylight.

John leaned forward. "There is a carriage coming up the drive."

Charlotte hurried to his side. The vehicle was large and cumbersome, drawn by four powerful bays. The coachman and footman wore livery of green and red with bright silver facings, the same colours as the crest painted ostentatiously on the door panels.

As the carriage drew up before the door, a tall, thick-set man stepped heavily down. He was as gaudily dressed as his servants, in a yellow waistcoat and green breeches, and a coat of purple broadcloth frogged with gold braiding in military style. His tricorne was exceptionally large, and his full white wig contrasted strongly with flushed cheeks and bright blue eyes. He bellowed at the footman, although the man was standing close beside him.

"Help Mr. Endacott down, damn you, Silas."

Charlotte turned to John. "I will go to the door and see . . ."

"We will both go." He took hold of her hand, smiling at her reassuringly. "At least your guardian is not dead."

Gervase was out of the carriage by the time they reached the door. His breeches and boots were caked with dirt, his hair loose, the ribbon missing. The sleeve of his coat was torn, his cravat bloodstained. Leaning on the footman's arm, he made his way towards the house. At sight of Charlotte, he thrust the man aside and asked anxiously, "You are unharmed?"

"Yes, thanks to Mr. Standish. But you . . . ?"

"It is nothing. Merely a few bruises." He gritted his teeth. "Charlotte, this is Sir William Ransom, my neighbour, who was good enough to bring me home. Sir William, may I present my cousin from Massachusetts, Miss Charlotte Endacott. And Mr. Standish, also from America."

The big man swept off his hat and bowed with as much gallantry as his burly figure allowed.

"Your servant, ma'am. And yours, sir."

After acknowledging his greeting, Charlotte turned towards the house. "I will fetch Mrs. Yeo."

"There's no need to make any fuss on my account," Sir William declared. "I'm not staying and I've already plied Endacott with as much brandy as he can take for the moment. Never was much of a drinker, not like his brothers. They drunk me under the table more than once, which takes some doing, I assure you."

John stepped forward, proffering his arm. "If you will allow me, Mr. Endacott."

Gervase declined John's assistance. He straightened with an obvious effort. "Again I thank you, Ransom. Your arrival was most timely, especially as my horse took fright and bolted."

The big man grunted. "My arrival wasn't timely for those murdering devils, though. I'll not need any evidence to have them strung up on the gallows or sent to the colonies. Saw it all with me own eyes, damn me if I didn't."

Gervase said wearily, "I have already told you. I wish no action taken. They had their reasons for attacking me. They believe that I . . ." He passed a hand across his forehead. "Forgive me, I am not able to think very clearly. But I tell you this, Ransom, I do not want them punished."

Sir William's face flushed an ever deeper red. "What *you* want is neither here nor there. You seem to have forgotten that I'm a magistrate, and whether you like it or not, I've my duty to do. And now, by your leave, and yours, ma'am,"—he bowed perfunctorily to Charlotte, "I'll return to Tiverton and attend to it."

Gervase stretched out a hand to stop him, then swayed and closed his eyes. Reluctantly he grasped John's arm. "In the morning," he murmured weakly. "Leave it until the morning."

"Better get him inside," his rescuer said to John.

"Yes, take him in, please," Charlotte added. She turned to Sir William. "Regarding the men who attacked him, I am sure my cousin would wish . . ."

"I know well enough what he wishes," he broke in. "But we're not all milksops like Endacott. If a horse throws you, you beat him. If a dog bites you, you shoot him. And if a mob of ignorant labourers sets upon you,

you string 'em up. That's common sense. That fellow," he jerked a thumb towards Gervase's retreating back, "was born without any, it seems. But there, as you've doubtless heard by now, the real *men* in your family are all dead."

Charlotte faced him, her head held high. "That, I think, sir," she said icily, "is a matter of opinion."

He stared down at her, his blue eyes wide. "You don't mean to say you agree with his views? I'm all in favour of tossing a guinea or two to the poor now and again, but if you give those fellows an inch . . . But there, why should I try to explain it to you? You're only a woman, after all, and from a country where half the inhabitants are heathens, so I'm told." He prepared to mount the steps, then turned back to her again. Wagging a thick finger at Charlotte, he declared solemnly, "You mark my words, miss. The ideas of men like Endacott'll only bring ruin to this country. If you've any sense at all, you'll refuse to listen to 'em. Good-day to you, ma'am."

The carriage lurched and its springs creaked as he entered it. The footman, with a daring wink at Charlotte, slammed the door and sprang up behind as, with the coachman's whip cracking above their backs, the horses lunged forward. Gravel scattered from hooves and wheels as the carriage swung round in a tight semi-circle and charged down the drive.

In the hall, Gervase sank down on a settle. "I will sit for a few minutes. I seem to have wrenched my back, which makes walking somewhat difficult, and the stairs . . ." He glanced upwards, frowning. "That's where it all started," he said, as if to himself, "on those stairs."

Mrs. Yeo came hurrying from the kitchen, wiping floury hands on her apron. She stopped short at sight of Gervase.

"Oh, sir, what a state you're in! The wicked devils! You must . . ."

As she went to him, he rose unsteadily to his feet.

"Let me be. A few hours' rest is all I need. Send Thomas to me."

"Thomas went to find you, sir, with Benedict. They must have passed you on the road, not realising you were in Sir William's carriage. Will I send the boy to help you?"

John stepped foward. "If you will allow me . . ."

Gervase forced a smile, and put a hand to his back. "Thank you. It's so devilish stiff. Charlotte, there is no need to look so anxious. I shall be perfectly all right by morning. I *must* be. Otherwise, those poor fellows will be . . ." He rubbed a hand across his forehead. "Ransom's brandy is such damned heady stuff, it stops a man thinking. I'd best get to bed and try to sleep it off."

Charlotte stood beside Mrs. Yeo as John helped Gervase up the stairs. At the turn, Gervase hesitated, then gritted his teeth and trod firmly on the stairs which previously he had skirted. Then he stopped and called down to his housekeeper.

"Bring me up some writing materials, and tell the boy to be ready to ride into Tiverton and deliver a note to the Mayor as quickly as he can."

"But, sir," Mrs. Yeo said anxiously, "there's not a riding horse in the stables. Yours, and the grey Miss Endacott was riding, haven't returned, and Tom and Bendict took two, and the chestnut has an injured fetlock, so Benedict told me."

Gervase leaned over the banisters. "Then tell the boy to take a carriage horse, or an ox or a goat or a sheep. But get to Tiverton he must, in time to stop Ransom . . ."

"Surely I can help?" John broke in. "I have a horse here, and I know where the Mayor lives."

"That's very kind of you, Standish, but it may involve you in some unpleasantness."

"I am already involved, I would remind you, sir, by rescuing your cousin. Besides, I can scarcely believe that delivering a note can have any undue consequences."

"Very well," Gervase said resignedly. "I am obliged to you."

When Mrs. Yeo had sent a maidservant up with paper and pen, she went towards the kitchen.

"Whatever the master says," she remarked to Charlotte, who was waiting for John to come downstairs, "he should be poulticed. I must see that hot water and unguents are ready for when Thomas returns, for the days are over when Mr. Gervase would let me tend him."

Charlotte put a detaining hand on the housekeeper's arm. "Mrs. Yeo, what happened on that staircase? Why does Mr. Endacott avoid stepping properly on certain stairs?"

The housekeeper looked taken aback. " 'Tis not a story he likes repeated," she said doubtfully. Then her face cleared. "But in view of what's happened, and seeing you're a member of the family . . . 'Twas a long time ago, nigh twenty years I'm thinking. Mr. Gervase was no more than a lad of six at the time. There was some fault in the panelling on the staircase and the master—Mr. Gervase's father that was—called in the best carpenter from Tiverton, Sam Biddlecombe. Mr. Biddlecombe said 'twould need doing one way, and the master, he said another, and they stood there arguing on the stairs. Leastways, not exactly arguing, for the master was shouting and waving his arms and the carpenter, he held to his point, quiet like but determined." She pursed her lips. "The master, of course, wouldn't stand for anybody's opinion but his own. Always right he was, or thought he was. But Sam Biddlecombe knew his job and wouldn't budge from what he held to be the way of it. Then the master raised his fist—'twas in temper, ma'am, not meant to do any real harm. But he caught the carpenter off balance and he fell backwards down the stairs, hitting his head on a statue that used to be at the corner—Mr. Gervase had it removed when he became master here."

"And the man was killed?" Charlotte asked in dismay.

"That's right, ma'am. The master couldn't believe it and started poking at Mr. Biddlecombe with his boot, ordering him to get up. Then Biddlecombe's son, a lad of fifteen who was apprenticed to his father, rushed up the stairs and started kicking at the master, telling him to leave the poor man alone. There was a rare to-do then, with the servants pulling young Biddlecombe off the master, and carrying his father away, and the mistress having hysterics and Master Gervase . . ."

"Yes?" Charlotte prompted. "He was there, too?"

"Aye. He saw it all. He just stood there, white as a sheet, his eyes as big as saucers. I didn't like the look of him, so I called the nurse and she took him away. Sick as a dog he was she said and she couldn't get him to sleep that night. He's never talked about it, not from that day to this, but always he avoids treading on the place where the carpenter died."

"And the man was called Biddlecombe, you said? The same name as the man who was found dead in the river?"

"Aye," the housekeeper said again, nodding her head. "That was Kit Biddlecombe, Sam's son, him as come back from the convict settlement a few days since, vowing he'd have his revenge."

"For the death of his father?"

"That, and his own punishment. Twenty years' transportation they gave him, for attacking the master."

"He did not harm Mr. Endacott, surely? You said the servants pulled him off."

"So they did, before he could do the master any injury. But he meant to, and that was enough for the magistrates."

"He was only fifteen," Charlotte protested, in dismay, "and he had just seen his father killed."

The housekeeper's face was without expression, her voice without emotion.

"He was naught but a carpenter's son, ma'am, a common labourer, and he attacked a gentleman. He was lucky not to be hanged. And now, if you'll excuse me, I'd best see about preparing the poultices, and putting on some gruel for Mr. Gervase."

Charlotte was still standing where Mrs. Yeo had left her, trying to visualise, with the eyes of a six-year-old boy, the scene which the housekeeper had described, when John came down the stairs, Gervase's letter in his hand. Without haste he picked up his hat and turned to her.

"Miss Charlotte, I would like to say that . . ."

"Not now, please," she entreated. "Ride as quickly as you can, I beg you."

"Why this anxiety on your part? Even if Sir William Ransom has his way, those men will scarcely be hanged out of hand. It will do them no harm to cool their hot heads in the bridewell."

Charlotte twisted her fingers together. "You are right, of course. But—but you see, like Gervase, I do not wish our name to be any more reviled than it is already. I have just learned of one more reason why our family is so hated."

Taking her hand, John looked at her with concern. "I wish I had the right to take you away from Stokeleigh. Do not become too involved in your guardian's affairs, Charlotte. Your future is not here, nor anywhere in England." He pressed her fingers. "Now I will do your bidding and race the wind to Tiverton. There, does that satisfy you?"

She smiled up at him. "Yes, indeed, and thank you. You are very kind, and very—understanding. Without you near at hand . . ."

"That possibility need not cause you a moment's anxiety. If my patron desires me to make an exact copy of

Blundell's School, I will do so, though it should take me six months or more!"

Gervase, walking, with the aid of a stick, along the landing, halted at the unfamiliar sound of a woman humming softly. It came, he discovered, from the little room which had been his mother's sitting-room, at the back of the house. Curious, he glanced inside.

Charlotte was sitting beside the window, her head bent over some sewing. Gervase stood out of sight, listening. The tune was like no other he had ever heard, plaintive, a little monotonous. Charlotte stopped to bite off a thread, a procedure his mother would have frowned upon; then held the needle to the light to re-thread it. Her profile was outlined against the distant woods. For the first time Gervase noticed how her eyelashes curled, how small her ear looked; how soft and shining her brown hair. There was colour now in her cheeks and lips and she wore a charming, if not very fashionable, gown of green muslin. He remembered how his mother had appeared, sitting in that same chair; stiff-backed, angular, with a reproach ready to utter the moment he entered her sanctum.

He had not been in that room since her death. Nor had anyone else, he supposed, save the maidservants who cleaned it. Yet this girl he had first thought so dowdy and meek, had seemingly taken possession. His mother's sewing-box was open on the table beside Charlotte, a shawl trailed untidily over a stool. The shutters were drawn back, the window open. Sunlight shone on Charlotte's hair as she plied her needle industriously. Gervase could scarcely believe his eyes.

Charlotte pushed hard at the needle, then, with a little cry, dropped her sewing. As Gervase hurried forward, she looked up, sucking her pricked finger. Recognising the garment laid across her lap, Gervase stopped short.

"That is my coat. Why are *you* mending my coat?"

"Why not?" she asked. "I am quite adept with a needle, though you might not think so at this moment."

"Charlotte, that is not a task for you. I employ a sewing-woman. Here, take my handkerchief."

Unfolding it, she pulled a face. " 'Tis somewhat large, I fear. If you would be kind enough to pass me my reticule from off the sofa . . ."

She produced a scrap of cambric and wound it round her injured finger. "Your mother's thimbles, like your handkerchief, are all too big. They kept falling off, so I did without one."

"We will buy one to fit you when we are next in Tiverton. But Charlotte, I beg you . . ." He stopped at sight of the determined lift of her chin, the glint in her blue eyes.

"I am sorry, cousin Gervase, but I can no longer remain idle in this house. It may be all very well for ladies brought up to a life of leisure, but it irks me to see tasks which neeed doing and be always prevented from undertaking them. I noticed yesterday that your coat had been torn, so I asked Thomas to bring it to me, and one of the maids to show me where I might find a sewing-box. I am sorry you are displeased, but I intend to finish it now that I have started."

Charlotte looked closely at him. "You have recovered from yesterday's misfortune?"

"I am somewhat stiff and bruised, nothing more. I deeply regret you were forced to witness such a scene, and to be involved in some unpleasantness, according to Mr. Standish."

"They thought you had killed Kit Biddlecombe, the carpenter's son your father had transported."

"How do you know about that?"

Charlotte snapped off a thread. "I have been greatly puzzled by your strange behaviour at the turn of the staircase. I questioned Mrs. Yeo. She was loath to tell me the story, but eventually she did so. I wish that you would be more truthful with me, Gervase. You lied to me about the night Kit Biddlecombe died, and you said things which were bound to arouse my suspicions, however much I did not want to suspect you of—of causing a man's death."

Sighing, he said, "Yes, I can see I acted very foolishly, and it was unfair to you. But, Charlotte, you do not suspect me any longer, do you? You do believe me when I say I had no hand in that poor fellow's death?"

Her eyes were clear and untroubled as she answered him. "Yes, I believe you, Gervase. And I am beginning to understand you, I think. But why did you say you were ashamed of what you did that night?"

He rose and went to the window, gripping the sill. "Because—because I acted contrary to my beliefs. I believed that Kit Biddlecombe had come to take my life, that he sought the revenge he had promised himself through twenty years of hell."

"But *you* did not kill his father. You were only a child."

He swung round to face her. "Do you suppose that mattered to him? The man whose life he sought was already dead. I was an Endacott, and living. That was enough for him."

"So you went out, alone, to face him?"

He avoided her eyes. "I went out, yes, and alone. But I armed myself with a pistol."

"Which any sensible man would have done."

"I had not intended to defend myself." Seeing her look of incredulity, he strove to explain. "Not with a weapon, I mean. I thought, if I faced him, unarmed, we could have talked. I could have made him understand that nothing could be gained by further bloodshed. That, given time, I would try to right some of the wrongs done to him and his kind."

Charlotte laid down her sewing. "You would deliberately have risked your life in the faint hope that his man would listen to you?"

Dejectedly he nodded.

"But you changed your mind," she reminded him. "Why?"

He stared unseeing at the distant woods. "You may find this difficult to believe, but it was because of you. While I was sitting beside the window, deciding what I should say if Biddlecombe did turn up, you came along the passage, looking very young and frightened. It occurred to me that if I were to die, so soon after Uncle Matthew, you would be left quite alone again, with no provision made." He clenched his hands. "At least, that was what I told myself was the reason for fetching the pistol."

Charlotte put aside his coat and came to stand beside him. "And now you are doubting that reason? I think you spend a great deal too much time in self-questioning, Gervase. What happened in the garden?"

"Nothing. Nothing at all. I waited for a very long time, but Kit Biddlecombe did not come." He sighed heavily. "We know why, now. Because he was already dead. I can only suppose that he had drunk hard to give himself courage, and leaned too far over the bridge." He turned to her and smiled ruefully. "So you see, my resolve was not even put to the test."

She looked levelly at him. "If it had been, I would not have had you weaken on my account."

He was suddenly very aware of her nearness, of some pleasing fragrance quite unlike the heavy perfume Sophia used. The room itself seemed to have taken on a different atmosphere because of her presence. It occurred to him that this should be a room to which a man might come, when he was weary or beset by problems, for the purpose of seeking ease and comfort in the company of his wife. Provided, of course, his wife were . . .

Sophia's voice cut across his thoughts. He started guiltily, and his practised self-assurance was lacking as he hastened across the room to her.

She brushed aside his greeting and nodded perfunctorily at Charlotte. "I am gratified to find you on your feet, Gervase. I have been told some extraordinary tale of your having been set upon by ruffians yesterday and all but murdered."

"It was not as bad as that," Gervase protested, pulling forward a chair, which Sophia ignored.

She was dressed in yellow, with red ribbons threaded through the lace at her elbows. A straw hat, decorated with artifical fruit, was tilted at a provocative angle on her dark hair. As usual, he paid mental tribute to her handsome appearance, but he wished she had not come. He had been feeling so at ease, talking here quietly with Charlotte.

Sophia pulled off her gloves. "I heard also that Will Ransom rescued you."

"That is true. He was driving up Gold Street in his carriage."

"And saw what happened?" As Gervase nodded, she declared with satisfaction. "Then there will be no time lost in punishing the rogues. If the matter were left to you, one could suppose they would escape with the merest warning, but we can safely leave Will to administer proper justice."

"Sir William administers the law," Gervase said stubbornly. "That is not necessarily the same as justice."

Sophia raised her dark eyebrows. "You had better not let him hear you make such a remark."

"Why not?"

"*Why not?* Gervase, I declare there are times when I believe you to be deliberately stupid and obstinate."

They could have been his mother's words, heard so often in this room. He had noticed before how Sophia resembled his mother in her choice of words. He had often wondered if she would become shrewish in middle age.

With difficulty he brought his attention back to what she was saying.

"Sir William would be most upset by such a calumny."

Gervase shrugged. "I doubt it. He has sufficient vanity and self-esteem to ignore remarks which smack of criticism."

"He is a man of bold character, with a strong sense of duty," Sophia retaliated. "I cannot conceive that *he* would ever be set upon by a mob of drunken labourers."

"You are right," Gervase agreed. "But then, why should he be? The Ransoms have not reduced hundreds of men and women to misery, not supposedly killed a man for wishing to avenge his father."

"Gervase, you are impossible!" Sophia flicked her gloves over a small oval table. "Why, you cannot even see that your servants perform their duties properly. Look at the dust on here." She glanced round the room with distaste. "I shall have this room altered entirely. The colours are altogether too insipid." She crossed to where Charlotte was sitting, quietly stitching. "May I ask what you are doing, Miss Endacott?"

Charlotte glanced up, smiling. "Mending Gervase's coat. See, the sleeve was torn in the struggle yesterday."

Sophia's mouth curved downwards. She pinched in her nostrils. "I should have thought . . ."

Gervase broke in quickly, "It is very kind of Charlotte to take such trouble, is it not?"

Sophia looked at him, a long, calculating look, and then at Charlotte's bowed head. When she spoke, her voice was as cutting as a knife.

"I drove over especially to ascertain if you were injured, Gervase. Surely the least return I may expect is the offer of some refreshment?"

They were sitting on the terrace, drinking chocolate, with Thomas standing deferentially at Sophia's elbow, when John Standish cantered up the drive. Charlotte half rose to greet him; then, catching Sophia's glance, sat primly with her hands in her lap until he joined them.

"There's a fine to-do in Tiverton this morning," he exclaimed after he had been presented to Sophia. " 'Tis said the gaolers were bribed to release the men who set upon you yesterday, Mr. Endacott, and the magistrates and constables are furious. Sir William Ransom is galloping round the town, cracking his whip and blowing on a hunting horn, for all the world as if he's after a fox instead of men."

Sophia clapped her hands and laughed. "How splendid! I shall drive in at once and see the fun." She rose, snatching up her reticule. "You will accompany me, Gervase?"

He got stiffly to his feet, wincing a little. "It will scarcely surprise you if I beg to be excused. After all, you have long since learned that we do not share the same ideas of what constitutes fun."

The colour rose in her cheeks, her dark eyes flashed. She tapped her foot on the gravel. Gervase saw open admiration in John Standish's eyes.

"You are too namby-pamby for words, Gervase," she flung at him, then turned to John. "May I prevail upon you to ride back beside my carriage, Mr. Standish?"

He made her a formal bow.

"Nothing would give me greater pleasure, ma'am. But I am not, unfortunately, a gentleman of leisure like Mr. Endacott. I came here this morning to discuss some business with him."

Sophia stood very straight, smoothing her gloves. "I see," she said with cold dignity, "the one has time and no inclination; the other inclination but no time. Doubtless I shall find Sir William will have abundance of both." She slipped the string of her reticule over her wrist. "I leave you to your dull discussions. And you, Miss Endacott, to your sewing, a most worthy occupation, I declare. No, do not trouble to accompany me to my carriage, Gervase. Doubtless your footman will do so with more eagerness."

Gervase shrugged and motioned Thomas to go with her. He saw that John's gaze followed Sophia until she entered her carriage and was out of sight. He saw that Charlotte was watching John, a tiny frown puckering her forehead.

He said, "Mr. Standish, am I to understand from your remark that you rode over to discuss the construction of the cottages which I spoke to you about in Tiverton?"

"Yes, that is so. There is some special gathering at the school today which makes it difficult for me to work there. I thought that if I could inspect the site you have in mind, and have a look at the cottages as they stand ..."

"By all means." Gervase sat down, pulling a face, a hand pressed to the small of his back. "I think you will have to go down without me, though. I am still finding walking difficult, and the thought of mounting a horse does not fill me with delight at present." He glanced at Charlotte. "Why do you not walk along the river path, which is a pleasant way of reaching the village, and take my cousin with you?"

Charlotte rose, smiling happily. "I will go and change my shoes. These are not suitable for rough walking."

"In the meantime, Standish," Gervase said, "I can explain to you the lie of the land." With his walking-stick he began to trace a plan of the riverside cottages and the land behind them.

John sat beside him, clasped hands between his knees. "Yes, I understand roughly what you want," he said; then went on hurriedly, "But before we go into details, Mr. Endacott, there is another matter I wish to discuss with you while Charlotte is out of hearing."

Charlotte walked happily beside John along the river path. A heat haze shimmered over the fields, and swallows skimmed the water, chasing the myriads of insects beneath the overhanging trees. John was bareheaded, his drawing-board under his arm. He held Charlotte's hand, helping her over the rough places and exposed tree roots. She felt no need to peer suspiciously amongst the trees or glance over her shoulder at every crack of a twig. For even if there had been danger, John was there to protect her.

He was so much easier a companion to be with than Gervase. His nature, it seemed to her, was open and uncomplicated; he had none of Gervase's self-doubt.

"I hope I may satisfy Endacott with my designs for these cottages," he said. "The terms he offers are most generous. Besides, it would be my first real commission —with a free hand, I mean."

"You still have no enthusiasm for this school you are working on?"

He shook his head. "A man should forge ahead by virtue of his own ideas if he is to make his mark in the world. And that is what I intend to do, as I have told you. But not in England. They are too traditional here. Besides, I do not care for what I have seen of the English, they are too arrogant. I long to return home and join in the struggle for independence and self-government instead of the present iniquitous system of being dictated to by a Parliament in London which has no conception of our problems."

"Such talk is beyond me, I fear," Charlotte confessed. "But I would dearly like to understand about such matters."

"And so you shall," he assured her, giving her hand a squeeze. "I will explain it all to you, for you have a lively intelligence. But I must not spare the time now. Your guardian is paying me handsomely even for this survey of the village, and although he is an Englishman, I intend to give him full value for his money."

They walked on for a little in silence. Then Charlotte said reflectively, "I begin to understand him better now. There is a contradiction in his nature which I think stems largely from his childhood. It seems that he knew little happiness or affection during those years. And, in truth, I cannot see that there is much likelihood of his having a great deal in the future."

John looked at her enquiringly.

"I mean, in his marriage," she explained.

John laughed shortly. "In that I would agree with you. They are most unsuited, I should say, and their marriage a ship which looks all set to founder before 'tis even launched."

She glanced sideways at him. "Yet you admired Miss Pendleton, I think."

"Certainly I did," he answered at once. "A man would need to be blind not to do so. She is a handsome woman with a fine, proud bearing."

"Would you have liked to accompany her to Tiverton, as she suggested?"

John stopped and looked searchingly at her. "Are you jealous, Charlotte? Ah, you are blushing, and it becomes you very well. The thought of Miss Pendleton's company had a certain attraction, I must admit, but if I accompanied her anywhere it would be at my inclination, not hers. She may have Endacott on leading-strings, the more fool he, but I'm not of the same stamp at all."

To her surprise, Charlotte found herself rising to Gervase's defence. "She does not have all her own way with him. A few days ago she left Stokeleigh at his bidding, albeit she was in a great tear. And you will recollect he did not go with her to Tiverton as she wanted."

"That is easily explained," John said airily. "He said himself it is difficult for him to move around at the moment. It is why he is not with us now."

Charlotte remained silent. She had her own ideas of why Gervase had suggested that she went with John while he looked at the cottages. It was yet another opportunity for them to become more closely acquainted, which might bring nearer the day when John would take her off her reluctant guardian's hands. She was beginning to feel sure that day would come. Why else should John pay her such attention and speak so freely of his future plans? Why should he promise to tell her of developments in America if he did not expect her to have some part in them? He had even declared that her future did not lie in England, and expressed the wish that he had the right to take her away from Stokeleigh.

The tiny doubt which had entered her mind when she saw his obvious admiration of Sophia, disappeared. Impulsively she pressed his fingers in a spontaneous gesture of gratitude and affection.

He turned and smiled warmly at her.

"Endacott's misfortune is my gain. I much prefer to have you to myself." He glanced along the path. "If we were not within sight of the village, I would be greatly tempted to kiss you."

Hastily she withdrew her hand. "I pray you will do no such thing. I suffer enough already from the unfriendly curiosity of the villagers."

John laughed. "Is that your only reason for objecting? You are blushing again, I see. You accomplish it much more prettily now than four weeks ago. Then, you went quite scarlet with embarrassment."

"It is most unkind of you to remind me," she said putting her hands to her cheeks. "And I do not 'accomplish' it, as you put it. 'Tis a twist of nature which causes me much annoyance."

He was still laughing. "I dare swear Miss Sophia would not blush at mention of a kiss. She'd the more likely be only too eager, and return it in full measure."

Charlotte stopped and stared at him in amazement. "How can you say such a thing? Miss Pendleton is a lady of good family and careful upbringing."

John threw back his head and laughed even more loudly. "I' faith, Charlotte, you do not suppose that would stop her? I'll wager that beneath that haughty air, Miss Sophia is as ready as any innkeeper's wench. There, now I have shocked you."

"Yes, you have," she admitted. "Not by your words,

but by their application to Miss Pendleton. I had not thought . . ."

"Of course you had not. She scarce addresses a word to you, does she? Yet I'll be bound she has a watchful eye on you."

"On *me?*"

"Yes, my dear Charlotte, on you. Miss Sophia may have little regard for her future husband, but she's not the woman to play second fiddle."

"I do not understand your meaning," Charlotte confessed.

John tucked her hand beneath his arm. "You have too kind and unsuspecting a nature. It caused me some concern when we met in Exeter and you repeated to me what sounded like a most unlikely story told you by Endacott. I was wrong in doubting him, it seems, for I am assured his behaviour to you is most proper. But I vow I'm not wrong in my estimation of Sophia Pendleton. And," he added reflectively, "since she seems in no more haste to marry than is Endacott himself, it would be interesting to discover who . . ." He broke off, frowning. "Are those the cottages he wants pulled down?"

She looked ahead to where he pointed. "Yes, that row of six beside the river."

"They do not look in any danger to me," he observed. "Why, they are set back from the river bank which in itself surely offers sufficient protection."

"Gervase says the River Exe is very prone to flooding in this district," Charlotte explained, "and there is some talk of the owner of the land upstream diverting its course, to make some fish ponds, I think Gervase said."

"That would be Sir William Ransom. He lives for sport of one kind or another, so I've heard, and I suppose with a constantly ailing wife one can scarcely blame him. Certainly he was fulfilling the role of the English hunting squire this morning in Tiverton, save that he was chasing men instead of foxes."

99

"He sounds a horrid man, and I thought his appearance exceedingly vulgar," Charlotte said a little too primly, which made John laugh at her again.

Taking her hand, he walked on. "Come now, we must stop pulling the English to pieces and apply ourselves to work. At least, I must do so and you may offer any ideas which you think helpful."

This was what she had hoped for: that he would think of her as a helpmate as well as companion. At Stokeleigh, save for mending Gervase's coat, she had been made to feel so useless, not needed by anyone. For while Gervase might air his problems freely to her, there was nothing she could do to help him solve them.

John was studying the row of cottages. "If Endacott is determined to have them down, there is a deal of good material which could be used in reconstruction."

"Where would the people live in the meantime?" Charlotte asked.

He glanced admiringly at her. "You have a quick intelligence, Charlotte. That is a point which had not occurred to me."

She felt a glow of warmth at his words. "Perhaps there is an empty cottage which can be used by each family in turn, though I do not suppose they will take kindly to the idea. I have learned since being here that, on the whole, English people do not take kindly to change, even for the better. It is so very different from home where we constantly work towards improvement."

John turned to her. "You said 'home,' Charlotte. America will always be that to you, will it not?"

She bent her head. "I fear so. I am sometimes very homesick. If it were not for you. . . ."

He pressed her hand. "I am glad I make things easier for you. We can share so much, you and I. Very soon now I shall . . ." He broke off, staring over her head in consternation. "I' faith, I do not think we shall be welcomed in the village. I could do with a blunderbuss to face this virago."

A woman was bearing down on them, a huge, heavy-browed woman with voluminous black skirts, and a shawl tied over her straggly hair. In a voice as raucous as a crow's she demanded, "What do 'ee want?"

"I am here on Mr. Endacott's business," John answered. "In any case, you have no right to bar our path."

The woman stood her ground, arms akimbo. "You were looking at our cottages, and with a deal of interest, I'm thinking. Why?"

John answered resignedly, "Because Mr. Endacott has a plan for pulling them down."

"*What?*" The woman glowered at him. "You'm a 'foreigner' but I'm thinking I heard 'ee aright. Mr. Endacott's aiming to pull down our cottages, did 'ee say?"

"Yes, that is right," John affirmed, "but . . ."

The woman turned and beckoned with a brawny arm, shouting to her neighbours who were hanging back in their doorways. At her summons they came forward, and others with them, from cottages on the further side of the green. They ranged themselves across the path, grey-haired grandmothers, and young women with children at their skirts. Every one stood as their leader was doing, with feet wide apart, arms akimbo. Their mouths were tight-lipped, their eyes hostile, as they stared at John and Charlotte.

The big woman spoke to them in such broad dialect that Charlotte could not understand a word, but the growing amazement and anger on their faces was evidence of what she had said. They began to mutter amongst themselves.

"Tell them, John," Charlotte urged. "Tell them they are to have new homes, safer ones."

He stepped forward, hand outstretched. The leader of the women advanced on him, her first raised threateningly.

"Get back to Mr. Endacott, you and this young woman 'e calls 'is cousin from America, tho' none of us 'as 'eard of such afore. Get you back, I say, and tell un to come 'isself and say what you've just said. And we'll be ready for un, won't us?" She appealed to her companions, who muttered angry agreement and, following her example, raised clenched fists. "We thought un different, for a time, but he'm no different to the rest of the Endacotts. Killed a man, 'e did, a few nights since, just like his father afore un. And now you say he be going to . . ."

Charlotte tugged at John's sleeve. "Do explain to them."

John thrust his drawing-board firmly under his arm. "I'm damned if I will," he declared grimly. "My task is to design buildings, not argue with a mob of uncouth peasant women. That is Endacott's problem."

Seizing Charlotte's arm, he turned on his heel and hurried her back along the river path, leaving the group of women cackling triumphantly behind them.

"I am sorry," Gervase said, when he heard what had happened. "I should have gone myself."

"That you should," John declared irritably. He sat on the wall of the terrace and kicked his heel against the stonework. "I was never more embarrassed in my life. To be kept from my work by a crowd of hectoring women . . ."

"They were afraid," Charlotte broke in, "they thought they were to lose their homes entirely. If you had only explained . . ."

"What chance had I to explain? Why, we scarcely speak the same language. You have said yourself you do not understand the half of what they say."

"Standish is right," Gervase said patiently. "You need to understand these country people to communicate with them, and even then it is not easy. It is their nature to be suspicious."

"It was not only suspicion of us which made them hostile," Charlotte said. "Like those men in Tiverton, they think you killed Kit Biddlecombe."

Gervase sighed. "That is no more than I would expect. It can be proved a dozen times that he fell from the bridge, yet they will not believe it. But that is of small account compared with the anxiety I have caused them by my folly in not going myself and explaining about the cottages. As soon as I can move more easily, tomorrow probably, I will go."

"You are like to be met with cabbage stumps and clods of earth," John said truculently.

Gervase smiled. "I will take care to wear my oldest suit."

"I do not understand you, Mr. Endacott," John declared. "Do you never get impatient with people's ignorance, their stupid inability to listen to reason? I think you English are the most obstinate people, and your air of superiority is exactly what is causing us in America to . . ." He broke off in confusion as he caught Charlotte's startled glance. "I am sorry. I should not speak to *you* in such a manner."

Gervase leaned back and crossed his legs. "You may speak to me how you wish, Standish. I am entirely in favour of freedom of expression. It seems to me that if the representatives of the various colonies, and some members of our Government, could sit at a table together and quietly discuss the difficulties, instead of ranting loudly on the one hand, and sending troops on the other . . ."

"You have studied the American question?" John asked in surprise.

"Certainly." He turned to Charlotte. "Would you be kind enough to ask Thomas to bring out some wine?"

When she returned, the two men were deep in conversation. John's voice was vibrant and he used his hands to emphasise some of his points, thumping his clenched fist into his palm.

"So you see," he declared bitterly, "if it comes to a fight, the reasons I have outlined will be the cause of it."

"Yes, I do see," Gervase admitted, taking a glass from the tray which the footman was handing round. "But it would be a thousand pities if it does happen. Once such a fight started, who knows where it would end? Surely you have had enough of bloodshed, in your wars against the French and the Indians, without setting yourselves up against your fellow-countrymen? That is a terrible thing to contemplate. Heaven knows, we have suffered from it in this country. During the civil war there were divided loyalties in every town, every village. Even members of the same family found themselves on opposite sides. And the hatred *that* engenders does not end when the fighting stops. I think men take too swiftly to the sword."

John drained his wine. "You are cast in a different mould from me. I am easily roused to anger in a just cause."

"Every man thinks his cause is the just one," Gervase pointed out. "Perhaps it is a weakness in me, but I so often see both sides of an argument."

"I think it *is* a weakness, sir. For you must for ever be in doubt as to which course to take."

"You are quite right. Except that, fortunately, there are occasions on which I see my course quite clearly, such as today. I have not the slightest doubt that I must go down and face the villagers, as soon as I am able, however unpalatable the prospect." His tone was bantering. "I dare swear you would advise me to go armed with a pair of pistols?"

John's eyes narrowed. "You are mocking me, I think. I do not take kindly to such remarks."

Gervase cast a sideways glance at Charlotte, and raised his eyebrows very slightly. "You are too quick to take offence, Mr. Standish. I assure you, I was not offering the slightest reflection on your conduct in withdrawing before the combined wrath of the village women. I should have had more sense than to have submitted you and Charlotte to such an experience."

His words were quiet, his manner perfectly polite. Yet John flushed as he rose to his feet. Whether it was

Gervase's intention, Charlotte did not know, but there was no doubt that he had made John look small. And that, she felt instinctively, was not an experience that John Standish would relish or easily forgive.

VII

Sophia came again to Stokeleigh that afternoon, after John had gone. Charlotte and Gervase were in the drawing-room. Gervase had taken from the china cabinet a Dresden figure, which Charlotte had been admiring. He was explaining its finer points when Thomas appeared at the door.

"Miss Pendleton, sir, and Miss Rebecca Pendleton."

Sophia swept into the room, as colourful as usual in a green silk dress with pink ribbons and wide-brimmed hat tied under her chin with a large bow. She was followed by a thin, pale-faced girl who resembled her sister only in the darkness of hair and boldness of eyes.

"I have brought Rebecca to meet Miss Endacott," Sophia announced. "Rebecca, this is Gervase's second cousin from America. I pray you make your curtsey without toppling over as you so often do."

The girl came forward, glancing angrily at her sister. Charlotte held out her hand.

"I am happy to meet you, Rebecca."

The girl surveyed Charlotte from head to toe. "I hope you will pardon my curiosity, ma'am. I have never met anyone from *America* before."

The tone of voice, the expression of disdain on her pale face, were replicas of her sister's. The word "America," spoken in that way, could have referred to the depths of the African jungle.

Sophia said casually, "Rebecca was so disappointed at not joining her sisters in Norfolk that I thought it would be pleasant for her to stay with you for a short time, Gervase."

He turned from replacing the china figure. "With me? But, Sophia . . ."

"If you do not want me," Rebecca broke in, colouring, "now that you have this—this lady . . ."

Gervase said hastily, "You are always welcome, Becky. It is just that . . ."

Sophia swept aside his mild protest. "There is another reason. Miss Endacott, I believe, is anxious to have some means of usefully employing her time. The last governess we had proved most unsatisfactory. If Miss Endacott would be willing . . ."

"To teach Becky?" Gervase asked in astonishment. "Really, Sophia, that is scarcely . . ."

"A suitable occupation? Why not? It is, after all, a post usually offered to gentlewomen who find themselves in difficult circumstances—which perfectly describes you, does it not, Miss Endacott?"

Charlotte controlled her anger with some difficulty. "Perfectly, ma'am," she agreed coldly. "In fact, I had at one time contemplated seeking such a post. To have one offered me, on my own doorstep, so to speak . . ."

"Your own doorstep?" Sophia's laugh was wholly artificial. "What a very odd turn of phrase. Though, to be sure, I conceive that for the moment you do consider this your home. Gervase has ever had a great sense of duty and is most charitably disposed."

He stepped forward. "I am but carrying out Uncle Matthew's wishes towards Charlotte. There is no need for you to emphasise the unfortunate position in which she finds herself."

Sophia's dark brows lifted. "Unfortunate? I should have thought she would consider herself quite the opposite. I do not think you lived quite in this style in America, Miss Endacott?"

Rebecca tittered. Charlotte clenched her hands. "I have made no secret of the fact that we were poor and worked exceedingly hard. But so did everyone else in Maine. We helped each other and made our own entertainment and were happy enough until—until my father died. It was not my wish that I should come to England, and I would return tomorrow if I could. It may be that I *shall* go back, one day. In the meantime, I have not the slightest desire to be dependent on Gervase."

"Charlotte, please." As Gervase laid a hand on her arm, Charlotte caught the glint in Sophia's eyes. He turned to his fiancée. "If Becky wants to stay here, then she shall, and if Charlotte wishes to occupy part of her time in helping her with reading and writing or even French..."

"Do you speak French?" the girl asked in astonishment.

"Certainly, and I venture to think with a passable accent," Charlotte said coolly. "My father taught me. He learned the language when he was stranded at one time on the island of Saint Pierre which the French were allowed to keep after the Treaty of Paris."

Rebecca's eyes widened. She turned to her sister. "Did you know that, Sophia? Perhaps Miss Endacott *will* improve my education."

Charlotte glanced from one to the other of the sisters. She was not sure which she was likely to find the most provoking.

Sophia tossed her head. "I have quite enough matters with which to occupy my mind without bothering about what is happening on the other side of the Atlantic. I shall go and instruct Mrs. Yeo now, Gervase, and then be on my way. I have promised to call upon Lady Ransom. Poor soul, she grows weaker than ever."

"And *that* should cause you no distress," her sister remarked bitingly.

"*Rebecca!*" Sophia's voice was like a whiplash. "How many times must I tell you not to speak out of turn? I trust you will not give Miss Endacott the impression that you have been brought up quite without manners." She turned to Gervase. "Will you instruct Thomas to carry her portmanteau up to the room she occupied before?"

"I am afraid that will not be possible. Charlotte is occupying that room."

Sophia raised her brows, seemed about to protest, then shrugged. "Very well. We must put her in one at the back. Though, to be sure, I would have preferred it to be a warm one because of her chest."

Resignedly Charlotte said, "I am quite prepared to move, Miss Pendleton. As you have pointed out, this is your future home, not mine."

"It happens to be my house at present." Gervase had not raised his voice, but his tone was as determined as Sophia's. "Charlotte will remain where she is and Mrs. Yeo will have the ordering of where Becky is to sleep." He bowed slightly to Sophia. "I would not wish you to be detained when you are bent on so worthy an expedition as visiting a sick neighbour."

Sophia's eyes blazed. Her already high colour deepened. "Are you being deliberately rude, Gervase?"

He moved to open the drawing-room door for her. "No. Merely declining to have my household arrangements disrupted solely on account of your latest whim. I will see you to your carriage, Sophia. Give my regards to Lady Ransom."

Sophia flashed him a furious look as she flounced out of the room. Rebecca tittered, then hastily put a hand to her mouth. It seemed to Charlotte that there had been an undercurrent of meaning in the exchange which she did not understand. But it was none of her affair. She smiled at the girl.

"I hope we may become friends, Rebecca. Or do you prefer to be called 'Becky'?"

The child said angrily, "Only Gervase calls me 'Becky.' It is special to him."

"I see. You are fond of Gervase?"

The girl looked stubborn. "What has that to do with you?"

"Nothing, of course. But I would remind you of your sister's warning. Even in America little girls are brought up to be polite . . ."

"I am not a little girl," Rebecca protested. "I am twelve." She tossed her head. "Some girls are betrothed at twelve."

"Do you wish to be betrothed?" Charlotte asked in surprise.

The girl bent her head and scuffed the toe of her black slipper on the carpet. "No. Since it cannot be . . ." She looked up. "Were you very surprised at my arrival?"

"Naturally. We had received no warning . . ."

"Did you expect to be warned that Sophia was sending a spy?"

Charlotte stared at the girl in astonishment. "I have not the slightest idea of your meaning. But if, as it seems, we are to play the rôles of governess and pupil, I should be obliged if you would treat me with some measure of respect."

"Why?" asked Rebecca insolently. "You're only an orphan without a penny piece, Sophia says."

Charlotte gasped. "How dare you speak to me like that?"

"Why shouldn't I? It's true, what I said, isn't it? *And* I know why I've been sent here—to make sure you don't set your cap at Gervase."

Charlotte stepped forward. "Rebecca, I am not averse to using my hand on a child who is being insufferably rude. I assure you it is not a soft, ladylike hand."

The girl backed, her black brows drawn together. "Gervase would not let you strike me. He would be angry with you."

"I am prepared to risk that."

"I have a weak chest."

"And so must not be punished or reprimanded?"

"Oh, Sophia reprimands me often enough," the girl

exclaimed with a show of bravado. "But 'tis like water off a duck's back."

"So you are a law unto yourself? I think you will find it a very uncomfortable position to maintain in the world."

Gervase came back into the drawing-room. "Are you two making friends?" he asked hopefully.

Rebecca turned to him, clasping her hands around his arm. "I do not think Miss Endacott likes me, Gervase. She threatened to—to slap me."

He glanced at Charlotte with a look of amusement in his eyes. "Indeed? Then I can only suppose, since cousin Charlotte is the gentlest of young women, that you deserved it."

The girl stood back, staring up into his face; then looked from him to Charlotte. The colour rose to her cheeks, then drained away. Without another word she put her hands to her mouth, and, the tears welling in her eyes, ran from the room.

Rebecca did not appear at supper that evening. Mrs. Yeo, looking annoyed, told Gervase that the girl thought she had a slight fever and had better keep to her room.

"Should I go up?" Charlotte enquired.

"No, ma'am, I think not," the housekeeper answered crustily. "When Miss Rebecca's in this state 'tis best to leave her alone."

"But what upset her?" asked Gervase, sitting opposite Charlotte in the dining-room. "I cannot think that you would treat the girl with anything but kindess."

Charlotte avoided his eyes. "I am not prepared to tell you of our conversation, particularly since it is obvious you and Rebecca are fond of one another."

"I'm sorry for the child," he said, and turned to the footman standing beside his chair. "That will do, Thomas, we can manage now." When they were alone, he went on, "Becky has always been delicate. That she was raised at all is due to Sophia's determination. It is a difficult position, in any case, being the youngest of a family. I know only too well, though the charge can scarcely be levelled at me, as it is at Becky, of being spoiled."

"I should think it might well be true in Rebecca's case. At least, she does not take kindly to correction."

"Oh, is that it?" he smiled and said with amusement, "I surmise she is trying you out, Charlotte."

"In what way?"

He helped himself to cheese before he answered. "She is very like Sophia in some things. They both profess to want their own way and yet I suspect they need to feel some restraint put upon them. In fact I believe that Sophia would admire me the more if, when we are married, I laid her across my knee and soundly spanked her. But I am not that kind of man."

His words surprised Charlotte as much as John's had done. From both men she was receiving a picture of Sophia which did not fit at all with her own.

Remembering how sarcastically Gervase had referred to the errand which took Sophia from Stokeleigh, Charlotte asked, "What is the matter with Lady Ransom?"

"She has a wasting disease." Thoughtfully he selected an apple. "She is the last woman in the world who should be wife to Sir William. He is a hearty man, as you saw, and should have had a half-dozen healthy children by now. She has never borne him a child which lived above a day or two. He and I are at odds over many matters, but I have no fault to find in his treatment of his wife. Naturally, being the man he is, he seeks compensation elsewhere, but he is constant in the kindness and patience he shows towards Lady Ransom."

"Does Sophia visit there often?"

Gervase paused in the peeling of the apple. Then he answered casually, "Quite often. She is at her best with sick people. You find that difficult to believe."

"I find many things about her difficult to believe. But then, I have never met anyone quite like her before.

Nor anyone like Sir William—nor yourself, if it comes to that."

He stretched across the table and put a hand over hers. "Poor Charlotte, you must find life very difficult here. But at least Mr. Standish offers you a means of escape."

With annoyance she felt the colour rushing to her cheeks. "Oh, as to that . . ."

"You knew, of course, that while you were changing your shoes this morning, he asked my permission to pay his addresses to you?"

She jerked up her head. "No, he did not tell me."

Gervase looked surprised. "There was little opportunity, perhaps? The difficulty you met with at the village . . ."

"Yes, that was it," she agreed hastily, recalling how John had been about to kiss her when he realised they were in sight of the cottages; that he had been saying how much they might share, when the woman had confronted them. "Am I to understand that you gave your permission, Gervase?"

He held his glass of wine up to the light, slowly twirling the stem. "I told him that if you favoured him, I should raise no objection. Our relationship—that is, my being your guardian—still seems to me ludicrous, and it is quite impossible for me to feel like some cautious greybeard where you are concerned. Yet I am greatly concerned for your future, and wish that you should be happy in your marriage."

"And you are confident that I shall be, with John?"

He leaned forward. "What is more important, Charlotte—are you?"

"I am becoming increasingly so. We have a great deal in common. We come from the same country, our speech is similar. We both want a great future for America. There is so much I can do to help him."

"These are sufficient reasons for ensuring a happy marriage?"

Puzzled by his tone, she said, "I cannot see why you should sound so doubtful."

He put down his glass. "You have not spoken of love, or even affection. Yet once you told me you would not marry without that."

"Of course I have affection for him," she declared. "Surely the fact that you wish to help a man proves that you love him?"

"Does it?" Gervase pushed aside his plate and, putting his elbow on the table, leaned his chin on it and looked her full in the eyes. "You mended my coat, Charlotte. Was that not wishing to help me?"

The blood rushed into her face. She tried to think of a suitable answer, but could not.

Again he laid his hand over hers. "That was unfair. You were merely seeking a task with which to occupy yourself, were you not? In any case, any service you render me comes in quite a different category, I think, being due to your great desire for independence, and to your mistaken idea that I find acting as your guardian an irksome task. I will not deny that I sought at first to avoid the responsibility. Now I say in all sincerity, your presence is welcome in my house."

There was a mist along the valley the next morning. After breakfasting alone with Gervase, at which meal he seemed withdrawn and unusually silent, Charlotte went up to her bedroom to fetch a shawl. She was tidying her dressing-table, for she still could not get used to having a maid to do everything for her, when there was a tap on the door. Rebecca stood there, looking sullen.

"Gervase ordered me to ask your pardon," she said, glancing about her as she entered the room. "I suppose you told him what I said?"

Charlotte pushed a drawer shut with more force than necessary. "Indeed I did not! And I have no wish to receive an apology ordered by someone else. If you yourself do not realise how rude you were . . ."

Rebecca tossed her head. "I like being rude. It amuses me."

Charlotte faced the girl. "Rebecca, if you are to remain at Stokeleigh, I think we should understand one another. I am not a paid servant here. Nor am I prepared to tolerate your insolence."

The girl shrugged. Deliberately scornful, she fingered the inexpensive material of Charlotte's dressing-wrapper laid across a chair. Charlotte, about to remonstrate, hesitated and looked searchingly at Rebecca. The girl was very thin and her dark eyes looked over-large in the pale face. She had as wilful a mouth as her sister, but it was still childish.

Charlotte said calmly, "If you wish me to give you a little instruction, Rebecca, I am quite willing to do so. But it must be clearly understood . . ."

"French?" The girl's manner was still arrogant, but Charlotte saw a gleam of interest in the bold eyes.

"Yes, if you have any aptitude for it."

"Oh, I shall master it very quickly," Rebecca assured her. "I am much cleverer than Sophia."

Charlotte closed the lid of her dressing-table. "Mrs. Yeo thinks there may be some exercise books in the schoolroom. We will go there." At the door she turned and looked directly at her companion. "But I am warning you, Rebecca, we are going to have a lesson in French. We are not going to discuss your sister, or Gervase, or me. Is that understood?"

The girl returned her look, seemed about to show defiance; then reluctantly lowered her eyes.

"Yes, ma'am," she mumbled.

The schoolroom was on the second floor, at the back of the house. It smelt musty and damp, and Charlotte glanced ruefully at the empty grate. The sun would break through later, Gervase had assured her, but there was no sign of it yet. The trees in the garden dripped with moisture; the woods were hidden.

Rebecca opened a cupboard. "The books used to be

kept in here." She started back. "Ugh! Spiders! Will you get the books, please, ma'am? I am afraid of spiders."

"They will not hurt you," Charlotte assured her, rummaging in the cupboard. "You are fortunate if you have nothing worse to fear. In America we have really dangerous animals—wolves and bears, for instance."

"You can see bears in England," Rebecca told her. "But they are always on a chain so they cannot chase after anyone. Were you ever chased by a bear, or by wolves?"

"No. But I have heard wolves howling quite close in winter, and I have seen wild bears more than once."

The girl's eyes widened. "Were you very frightened?"

"Yes," Charlotte admitted. "But I was with my father and he was never without a gun in the woods. That is something I have had to grow accustomed to in this country—being able to walk out without fear of dangerous animals or Indians."

"*Indians?*" Rebecca repeated incredulously. "Have you really met Red Indians?"

Charlotte found an unused exercise book and an inkwell. "Often. But around Southport, where I used to live, they were most friendly."

The girl pulled a chair to the little desk. As she sat down she started to cough. It was a hard, dry cough, and she hunched her shoulders and pressed a clenched hand against her thin chest.

Charlotte asked, "Are you cold, Rebecca? Is that what makes you cough?"

The girl nodded. "It is because it is so damp this morning."

Charlotte made for the door. "I will see about a fire."

With a return of her former insolence, Rebecca exclaimed, "You said you were not a paid servant. Why do you not just pull the bell-rope?"

Charlotte paused, a hand on the door knob. "Yes, of course," she said, colouring. "Perhaps you will do it for me?"

Again the girl tried to stare her out; then rose and jerked at the tasselled rope hanging beside the fireplace.

It was the housekeeper who answered the summons. "My goodness, of course you need a fire in here. Why ever didn't you ask one of the maids, ma'am?"

"Because she was afraid to do so," Rebecca said airily. "Miss Endacott is not used to dealing with servants."

Mrs. Yeo swung round in the doorway. "I'll thank you to keep a civil tongue in your head, miss."

"And I'll thank *you* not to answer back," the girl retorted. "You're only the housekeeper here, and when my sister is mistress . . ."

"That day's not come yet, and I doubt I'll be here when it does. So 'tis no use trying your grand airs on me, young lady, and you needn't think Miss Endacott will stand for them either."

Rebecca stood her ground, feet planted wide apart, stomach thrust out, in a wholly childish posture. "I'll tell Mr. Gervase that . . ." Her words were cut off by another spasm of coughing.

"And 'tis not a bit of use you playing that trick," the housekeeper added grimly. "You've tried it on a time too many for me to be caught by it."

But Charlotte had seen something the housekeeper missed, the spot of red on the handkerchief the girl pressed to her lips.

"Thank you, Mrs. Yeo," she said quietly. "If we might have the fire lit as soon as possible."

When the housekeeper had gone, with a swish of black skirts and a quiver of her large white cap, Charlotte said, in the same quiet tone, "I think you had better sit down, Rebecca, and not talk so much. I will write you out a list of simple French nouns which you may learn by heart."

The girl plumped on to the chair beside the desk. When she had regained her breath, she broke out furiously, "My cough is *not* a trick. I really do . . ."

"I know." Charlotte took off her shawl and draped it around the girl's shoulders. "You had better borrow this until the fire is lit."

Rebecca said truculently, "You can't win me over by pretending to fuss me. I shall still report everything to Sophia."

Charlotte sat down at the desk as the young maid bustled into the room with a bucket of coal and some sticks. She picked up the pen and began to write. When she had completed the page, she handed the book to Rebecca and rose.

"I will tell you how to pronounce those words when I return," she said firmly. "In the meantime, you can learn the correct spelling and what they mean. I have written the English words opposite."

Rebecca half rose from her chair. There was fear in her eyes. "You are going to Gervase, to tell him . . ."

"I am going to my bedroom," Charlotte told her. "To fetch another shawl."

She was on the first landing when she heard the dogs barking, and a commotion at the front of the house. She went to the window which overlooked the terrace. A group of men stood below; rough-looking men, farm labourers, mostly, she thought. For they carried staves and pitchforks and scythes. Their voices were raised, and they looked as angry as the women of the village, as hostile as the woolcombers in Tiverton.

Charlotte retreated from the window and ran to look over the stairs. Gervase was coming out of the library. Charlotte called down to him. He stopped and glanced up.

"It seems I am forestalled," he said. "I should have gone down to the village yesterday evening."

As he continued across the hall, she asked anxiously, "You are going out to them?"

"Of course."

Bunching her skirts, Charlotte ran down the stairs and caught his arm. "Gervase, take care. You have not yet recovered from the woolcombers' attack and these men appear every bit as violent. You are surely not going to face them unarmed?"

"The sight of a pistol would rouse them to even greater anger."

"Then at least have Thomas and Benedict with you. You cannot go out there alone."

As he looked at her, the sadness in his eyes caught at her heart.

"My only hope is to win their confidence."

As he gently disengaged her arm, Charlotte said in dismay, "This is our fault, John's and mine. If we had only stayed to explain . . ."

He shook his head. "That was my responsibility, not yours. Now I must go and set their fears at rest."

Charlotte stepped forward. "I am coming with you."

"Charlotte, no." Gervase's voice was raised in protest.

She said again, determinedly, "I am coming with you, Gervase. They may regard me as a curiosity, but I am assured they will not harm me."

He moved to bar her way. "I forbid it, Charlotte. You will stay here, inside the house, where I know you are safe."

She wanted to argue, to force her way past him. But his eyes held hers, and his face was sterner than she had ever seen it.

"Very well," she conceded. "But I shall stay within call, and I shall have Thomas and Benedict with me, too."

When the front door had closed behind Gervase, Charlotte summoned the manservants, and with them and the housekeeper, she stood just out of sight beside the drawing-room windows.

"Open the window, Tom," Mrs. Yeo ordered. "So we can hear what's said."

Silent now, the men stood on the terrace, shuffling their feet, gripping their weapons with earth-stained fingers. Gervase confronted them, one hand negligently clasping the silver-faced edge of his grey silk coat, his attitude so relaxed he could have been paying a morning call. His voice carried clearly to the hidden listeners.

"I do not need to be told why you are here. But you have forestalled me. I intended coming down to the village this morning to explain the matter which is doubtless troubling you."

A big, swarthy man stepped forward, shaking the pitchfork he carried. "Aye, you'll explain it, we'll see to that." He made a sweeping gesture. " 'Tis a mighty fine 'ouse you 'ave 'ere. 'Tisn't likely this un will come down, is it? Though 'tis nigh as near the river as our cottages."

Gervase held his ground. "I have already said, Batten, that I am ready to clear up a misunderstanding. But I am not prepared to talk to you while you threaten me. You will put aside the staves and implements you are carrying. I cannot imagine why you thought it necessary to bring them."

"Can't 'ee?" The big man thrust his head forward. "I'll tell 'ee why us brought un. Last time us come to Stoke-leigh—on account of the land enclosure, it was, and us meant no 'arm—your father set the dogs on us. Big dogs they was, and fierce. My young brother's leg was ripped wide open. He's been lame ever since."

Gervase frowned. "Yes, I know about that. But I do assure you, the dogs are shut up this morning and will not be loosed. In any case, *my* dogs admittedly sound fierce enough, but they would not bite a man unless he provoked them."

"That be true, Joshua," a man at the back of the group called. "They other savage critturs was all got rid of when the old master died."

"Are you convinced now?" Gervase asked in the superior voice which had so irked Charlotte at their first meeting. He spread his hands before him. "As you see, I am myself completely unarmed."

119

"But you've servants," Joshua Batten persisted, "and I dare swear . . ."

"That there is a man with a blunderbuss hidden behind every tree; and the garden boy, with a bow and arrow, behind a chimney-stack?"

There was a guffaw from the man who had supported Gervase. Hesitantly, others joined in the laughter.

Gervase smiled. "So, unless you really intend to impale me on the prongs of a hayfork, you will oblige me by laying down your weapons. I find it somewhat disconcerting to address you while they are brandished before my eyes."

Sheepishly, the men laid at their feet the staves and billhooks. Batten was the last to do so. Eventually, grumbling, he flung down his pitchfork but kept his foot firmly upon it.

"Thank you," Gervase said, as casually as if he had merely asked them to throw their dice. "Now I will explain."

Charlotte sighed with relief. Thomas's eyes were wide with wonder. He shook his head in bewilderment.

"I don't know how he does it, that I don't. I've seed it happen afore. In Exeter, it was. We was down an alleyway and a lot of drunken fellows come on us and blocked our path. Any other man would have set about them with his cane, and there'd likely have been a deal of trouble. But Mr. Gervase just stood his ground and spoke to them, quiet as he be now, and dam me if they didn't step aside and let us through. Fair flummoxed me, it did."

" 'Tis his grandmother coming out in him," Mrs. Yeo said with satisfaction. " 'Tis something about the eyes. I can't rightly say what. I only know that, gentle as she was, I could never have faced Mrs. Willoughby if I'd done anything the least wrong." She tweaked her apron. "Now all the fuss be over, I'd best get back to my work. You too, Tom. There's the silver to clean."

After listening to Gervase's explanation, the men were

beginning to disperse, retrieving their assortment of weapons as if they would rather have disowned them, when the sound of hooves thudding up the drive reached Charlotte through the open window. The men hesitated; then scattered in confusion as a horseman galloped headlong on to the terrace. As he drew rein, forcing his mount on to its haunches, Charlotte recognised Sir William Ransom. His face was flushed, his wig awry. His mustard-coloured riding suit made him look bigger than ever.

"Heard you had trouble, Endacott," he shouted, flourishing his whip. "Came to your rescue—only just in time, by the look of it."

Gervase had not moved. He stood as if mesmerised, staring in consternation at his excited neighbor. Sir William pointed down the drive.

"Reinforcements arriving. We'll soon have these devils disarmed."

Gervase looked from Sir William to the men, then stepped forward and caught at the horse's bridle. "I do assure you . . ."

His words were cut off. Joshua Batten caught him by the collar, forcing him backwards. He held the prongs of the pitchfork within an inch of Gervase's throat.

"You devil!" he roared. "You treacherous, murdering devil! You'm no better than the rest of the Endacotts. Making us lay aside our weapons, so that us would be defenceless when your friends arrived. But they were a mite too late. Us'll make a fight of it, I promise you."

Sir William rose in his stirrups and shouted a halloo as six of his servants thundered up the drive.

"Corner them!" he yelled, his face crimson, his eyes shining with excitement. "No quarter!"

He swung his horse round. The handle of his whip cracked down on Batten's wrist. Bellowing with pain and fury, the big labourer dropped the hayfork.

Gervase, abruptly released, sprawled on the gravel.

His rescuer flung himself off his mount and stood over him, confronting the group of men. Charlotte saw the shocked amazement on their faces as they looked from their injured spokesman to Gervase, striving to rise from between Sir William's straddling legs. The magistrate, shaking his clenched fist, brandishing his whip, yelled orders to his servants. Nothing, it seemed, could stop a savage and bloody fight.

Charlotte made for the terrace by the quickest route—over the window-sill. She heard the rasp of torn material as her skirt caught on a bush. Wrenching it free, she ran forward. She flung herself at Sir William, pummelling at his massive chest with her clenched fists.

"Stop it! Stop it, you stupid blundering fool!"

She saw the magistrate's mouth drop open, his blue eyes widen in astonishment. Clutching the edges of his coat, she tried to force him backwards. As he gave way before her onslaught, Gervase rose and stood between them.

"Charlotte, please. Go inside."

"I will not!" She wrenched the whip from Sir William's hand and hurled it across the terrace. "Send your servants away," she ordered. "They are not needed here. Neither are you."

"How dare you!" Sir William expostulated. "I came here . . ."

Charlotte cut him short. "Gervase had dealt with these men without threats or violence. They were about to leave, peaceably, trusting him, when you rode up like a—a Red Indian chief on the warpath, spoiling everything."

As, speechless now he gaped down at her, she turned from him and, brushing aside Gervase's arm outstretched to waylay her, went to the injured labourer.

"Is your wrist broken? If so, I will attend to it. I am tolerably skilled at splinting broken bones."

The astonished man suffered her to run her fingers gently over the injury. Frowning heavily, he asked,

"Do 'ee mean to say, ma'am, that Mr. Endacott didn't summon Sir William, that this wasn't a plot to catch us unawares?"

"Of course it was not." She looked up into his face and saw the suspicion still there. "Can you really suppose that Mr. Endacott would have come out and faced you, alone and unarmed, if he had sent for help? Would he not have waited inside the house? Indeed, you are a fool if you cannot see that."

Batten gulped, then winced as her fingers prodded. Charlotte turned to Gervase.

"This wrist needs attention. Have I your permission to take this man into the kitchen?"

"My permission?" he repeated in a dazed tone. "You appear like a veritable tornado, whirling us all aside, and now, you ask my permission to . . ." He spread his hands in a helpless gesture.

The men from the village, still keeping wary eyes on Sir William's servants, began to titter. The servants joined in, their hands to their mouths so that their master should not see.

But Sir William had seen, and heard. His face grew almost purple, a vein throbbed at his temple. The knuckles showed whitely as he clenched his big hands.

"By heaven, you'll answer for this, Endacott," he thundered. "No one, man or woman, makes a fool of me and escapes the consequences." He flung out an arm. "This is a fine way, I must say, to treat a neighbour who came to your aid."

Gervase's tone was cold. "I am obliged for your thought, sir. But, as my cousin has told you, I did not need your aid. Nor do I wish for your intervention in what are entirely my own affairs. You have already done me great harm."

The magistrate thrust out his jaw. "How, may I ask?"

"By further antagonising the woolcombers in Tiverton. I sent word to the Mayor to have them released from gaol. That affair would have blown over, and I might in time have gained their confidence. But what must *you* do but hound them round the town as if they were vermin."

"And so they are! And more cunning than a pack of weasels—just as these devils are."

Joshua Batten made a move forward, but Charlotte laid a hand on his arm. "Leave it to Mr. Endacott," she warned.

Gervase was brushing dirt from his sleeves. "I shall be obliged if you will leave now, sir, and take your servants with you. These men's wives will doubtless be wondering what has happened to them."

Sir William, bidding one of his servants hold his horse and another to fetch his whip, mounted heavily. Ramming his hat more firmly on his head, he leaned towards Gervase.

"I'm warning you, Endacott, I don't take insults, especially from an arrogant popinjay like you. Or from foreign women." His gaze went scathingly over Charlotte. "It seems you aim to set up this ill-mannered chit in place of Sophia. You must be mad!" He wheeled his mount, shouting to his servants to follow. Over his shoulder he called back. "If you think I'll delay work on the river after this, you're mightily mistaken. I'll have my workmen start digging this very day. And if your miserable cottages, and even your own house, are flooded as a result, so much the better!"

Gervase went into the library and closed the door. For a few moments he stood in the middle of the room head bent, arms hanging limply by his sides. He felt his left palm growing wet, and glancing at it, was surprised to find it was bleeding.

If he were to go to the kitchen, Charlotte would attend to it as she was presumably attending at this moment to Batten's wrist. Her blue eyes would be filled with sympathy and concern. Her voice, which had been so recently raised in anger, would be quiet again, soothing.

Gervase took out his handkerchief and viciously jabbed at his palm, perversely glad of the pain. He strode across the room and jerked open the door of a cupboard. Carelessly tipping the decanter, he slopped brandy into a glass and drank it down, so rapidly he made himself cough.

What was he to say to this girl who was incredibly his ward? Ruefully he recalled that at first he had thought her plain and dowdy and meek. Yet not twenty minutes since, he had seen her scrambling over the drawing-room window sill like a hoyden; running, with her petticoat showing, across the terrace and attacking that meddling fool, Ransom, with her little fists; her hair falling loose, her cheeks flaming. He might have been watching a Punch and Judy show, save that he himself had been part of the performance. With disgust he remembered his own part, spread-eagled between Ransom's heavily booted legs. But the men, those simple men from the village whose emotions could be swayed in a moment—how they had loved it. Again he heard their laughter and saw the amazement and admiration on their faces, followed by relief as they loosed their grip on the primitive weapons with which they had armed themselves. Armed themselves against an Endacott, he reminded himself, in fear of what an Endacott might do in answer to their justifiable requests.

But he had shown them that they need no longer come in fear to Stokeleigh. Given time, he would convince them that his plans were for their good; as he would convince the woolcombers, weavers and spinners in Tiverton, that to be employed by an Endacott need not mean starvation wages, over-long hours, and bad conditions.

For the present, there was another problem to be solved, one that did not concern the village, or anyone in Tiverton—save John Standish. The problem of his own feelings; the temptation under his very roof.

Nothing that had happened in the last hour had so shaken him as Ransom's words: "It seems you aim to set up this ill-mannered chit in place of Sophia."

That, Gervase knew now, was just what he would do, given the slightest chance. He supposed he had partially realised his true feelings in his mother's little parlour. He had become more aware of them last evening when Sophia had so cruelly tried to belittle Charlotte. He was certain of them now, as he called to mind how she had come to his aid, regardless of dignity or propriety or danger.

"We have a great deal in common," she had said of herself and John Standish.

But had she not just as much in common with himself? Her anger at injustice, her concern for those who could not help themselves, her refusal to be provoked by scornful jibes.

"There is so much I can do to help him." To help John Standish, she had meant. But why not himself, just as she had done this morning?

But there was something else she had said, Gervase recalled with reluctance. "Of course I have affection for him."

Even if by some means he could transfer that affection to himself, what would be the use? He was not free. He was tied to Sophia.

Gervase pressed his handkerchief to his injured hand. By the sharpness of the pain, he realised there must be grit in the wound. The physical hurt matched his feelings and gave them some relief. He saw ahead of him the long years of his marriage. He saw himself and Sophia, neither bearing the other the least affection; she despising him, he pitying her because she would be his wife and not Henry's, when she became mistress of Stokeleigh. If Henry had lived . . . If Henry had lived, he himself would not now be at Stokeleigh and Sophia would have had no need to seek elsewhere for the nearest substitute for Henry. Gervase knew that he could never satisfy the kind of feelings she had shown towards his brother, openly physical, brazenly so at times, so that even his father had been a little shocked.

At least she had the decency to keep her present liaison moderately discreet. Becky was aware of it, Gervase felt sure. But he doubted if it had reached the village, or her father's ears. When he and Sophia married, he supposed he must take steps to end the affair, for a cuckolded husband was a laughing-stock. Until that time, it was best she had her way.

He picked up the decanter, tilted it, then set it down again. To drink himself into a stupor so that he need not face reality was weakness. All his life he had dreaded weakness above all else. Men like his father, or his brothers or Will Ransom could drink themselves under the table and be thought hearty, brave fellows. And men like that, or John Standish with his strong features and forthright speech and driving ambition—they were the ones to arouse admiration in a woman. But he himself . . . What sort of picture had he presented to Charlotte? Twice he had been sent sprawling in the dust before her eyes. He had allowed himself to be belittled by Sophia, almost argued to a standstill by John Standish. A sorry picture, surely?

So much the better then. For there would be not the least likelihood that Charlotte might prefer him to Standish. He was not free. He could offer her nothing. There was only one course for him to take: to keep a tight control on his feelings and encourage her betrothal to another man.

There was a soft knock on the door. Charlotte came in and stood hesitant, anxiety in her eyes.

"Gervase, I have come to ask your pardon. I think I behaved with . . ." She broke off, catching sight of his stained handkerchief. "Oh, you have hurt your hand. Let me see."

She went swiftly towards him. He wanted to open his arms wide and have her go straight into them. He wanted to hold her close and never let her go. Instead, he thrust his injured hand behind his back and spoke with deliberate coldness.

"It is nothing, I assure you. And as to your behaviour, any indiscretion is quite forgotten." He bowed slightly and went towards the door. "You will excuse me? I was just about to change my suit."

VIII

It became increasingly clear to Charlotte that Gervase was avoiding her. She felt hurt and rebellious. For, however imprudent her conduct had been, she had acted in that manner for one reason only, to help Gervase.

Small thanks she had received for her efforts. She had been made to feel as if she had behaved like a naughty child. Thomas had admonished her for not calling him to his master's aid. The maids' faces had been shocked and Mrs. Yeo's eyebrows expressively raised as Charlotte led the injured labourer into the kitchen. By evening, Rebecca had got hold of the story and taunted Charlotte.

"You think my behaviour unladylike, but I would have been severely reprimanded for clambering over a window-sill. And if I had torn my gown in such a manner, I vow Sophia would have put me on bread and water for days."

Feeling lonely and misjudged, and without Bella's comforting presence, Charlotte longed for John. She was sure *he* would not condemn her action. To him, as to herself, helping people was more important than paying strict attention to propriety. In his eyes, she was someone to be admired. Here at Stokeleigh, once again she had been made to feel inferior.

She endured as best she could the two days before John came. Mealtimes, with Gervase at the opposite end of the table and Rebecca between them, were an ordeal and Charlotte was thankful for Thomas's presence, which ensured that conversation was merely polite and casual. She would have welcomed Sophia's arrival, since the charged atmosphere of the house would doubtless have been relieved by an outburst on her part. But it seemed that Sophia had not yet heard of Charlotte's intervention on the terrace, for Charlotte could not believe that the older woman would miss such an opportunity for further censuring her.

John came at last, on the Monday afternoon, telling Charlotte that he had been catching up on his work at the school before giving any more time to Gervase's plans, and that he had spent Sunday with one of the masters at Blundell's School.

"There can be few Puritans amongst the merchants' wives in Tiverton," he declared. "For I never saw women more hung about with ribbons and gewgaws. They must spend as much time preparing for church as they do in their pews. They would certainly cause much adverse comment in Boston or Salem."

"There is so much that is different here," Charlotte agreed. "I find it strange, too, not to be within sight and sound of the sea."

He looked searchingly into her face. "You are unhappy, I think. Has Endacott been unkind to you?"

She shook her head. "He would not think so, I believe. It is simply that his moods change so quickly, I cannot follow them. One moment I appear to be in favour, the next in disgrace."

John frowned. "It is unpardonable that he should treat you in this way. You have suffered enough already. He should realise that, and be at some pains to make life happier for you, not to add to your distress." He thrust out his chin. "I will speak to him."

She laid a hand on his sleeve. "No, John please. It is kind of you to wish to—to protect me. But you have work to do for Gervase and I would not have my conduct prejudice him against you. I will tell you later what happened two days ago, and you may judge for yourself whether I am justified in feeling so resentful."

She walked in the garden while John and Gervase talked together in the library about the cottages. When John joined her again, his step was jaunty, his eyes shining.

"Endacott has increased his payment," he told her with satisfaction. "That is, provided I get on with the work at once. It seems that his neighbour has threatened to divert the course of the river sooner than expected, thereby increasing the danger to the cottages. Endacott is coming along to the village to show me where he plans to erect the new buildings. But he has some important matter to attend to for the moment and suggests that we go ahead of him. Will you need a cloak?"

"No, I think not," she said, again gratified by his thoughtfulness. "It is quite warm after the chill of the last two days."

This time they walked to the village by the lane instead of the river path. John's eyes were alert, noting the details of every building they passed. He drew her attention to their solid construction; to where, in the older ones, a room or two had been added by utilising what had been formerly the cattle shippens.

She laughed at him. "I thought you had no interest in old buildings."

"They are certainly not my choice. But when I am paid to design houses, or anything else, I must comply with my employer's wishes. And Mr. Endacott is insistent that these cottages, though he wants them to be more comfortable and convenient than the present ones, are to be in the same style as the rest of the village."

His tone was scornful. "He is no more open to progressive thought than any other Englishman I have met. In Tiverton they have had two disastrous fires, with much loss of life and property, yet I doubt if they have learned any lesson at all from such calamities. How I look forward to returning to America, where men's eyes are fixed on the future."

"You have scarcely seen anything of England yet," she pointed out. "Surely you wish to go to London?"

He shrugged. "The seat of the English Parliament? Where live the men who would impose their taxes and regulations on us without having the least idea of the colonists' problems. It might be better if I kept well clear of London, for fear I should make my views only too obvious and end up in prison as a traitor."

"Could that really happen?" she asked in dismay.

"I am sure of it. And that is not the way I intend to order my affairs. There is too much to be done in our own country for me to waste my time in arguing with block-headed Englishmen."

Amongst whom, Charlotte realised, he would class Gervase. She glanced up at him. He was looking straight ahead. The cleft in his chin was very pronounced, his mouth firm and uncompromising.

"Do you not see, Charlotte?" he went on, "what an exciting prospect is before us? To take part in creating a new world, a world of the future, not the past. As the colonies thrive and expand, there will be new communities, not only in Boston and Salem and all the other established towns, but in places we have not yet heard of." He turned to her. "Do you not want to be a part of that future, as I do?"

"Oh, yes," she answered fervently. And yet, somewhere at the back of her mind, a small voice questioned. "Are you sure?" Disconcertingly, she had a sudden inward picture of her mother, lovingly touching the few pieces of furniture and china which had come out from England. She heard Gervase's voice saying, "The Pendletons' house dates back to 1560, but I still consider it one of the most attractive buildings I have ever seen."

John said, "Charlotte, I think it is time I spoke to you of a matter which . . ."

His voice was drowned by loud bleating as a flock of sheep surged out of a field ahead of them and milled around them. Charlotte would have been knocked off her feet but for John's supporting arm as the animals ran in all directions.

A bent old man followed leisurely behind the sheep, chewing a piece of straw. John called to him.

"Why the devil can't you control your flock? They all but had this lady off her feet."

The shepherd moved the straw to the other side of his mouth and regarded John impassively.

"Sheep won't hurt 'ee," he answered imperturbably.

"They may not hurt her, but they have dirtied her gown," John declared indignantly.

Solemnly the old man regarded Charlotte's skirt. "The river's over yonder, for to wash un in," he pointed out reasonably. " 'Tis but a mite o' clean dirt, zur, 'tain't even proper muck."

As John was about to remonstrate, Charlotte broke in, "He is right, you know. These animals cannot have been shorn above a few weeks and look exceedingly clean. And nobody can really control sheep, can they? They are the silliest creatures."

"They'm not *that* silly, not when you knows 'em," the shepherd protested. "And I reckon *I* ought to know zummat about un. Been a shepherd all my life." He pointed across the river. His fingers were misshapen, the skin blotched. His hand shook a little. "Seen every kind o' weather on them hills. I've knowed springs when even the bird song was drownded by the call o' lambs. And others when 'twas as silent as the grave. Snow silence, I calls it. Not a lamb left alive, and the ewes in every kind of trouble."

John stepped forward, but Charlotte held him back.

She spoke to the old man, whose gaze was on the hills. "Go on with what you were saying. You must have seen many lambing seasons, I think."

"That I have. I don't rightly know the number of my years. I be as old as the springs and zummers I've known. That matters more than counting figures—never was much gude at that. And you don't need numbers to tell 'ee whether 'tis a good lambing year, nor one of they calendar things I've heard tell of, to know when 'tis summer or winter."

"Where do you live?" Charlotte asked. "In the village?"

He shook his head, jerking a thumb over his shoulder. "I've a place o' sorts over against the wood, beside the stream. Cob and thatch. 'Tis all I need. I be mostly upalong."

John was getting impatient. "Charlotte, we must not dawdle here. You seem to forget that it is Mr. Endacott's time we are wasting."

The old man caught at the name. "There's a man as would 'ave made a gude shepherd, if he'd been born different. He lets sheep take their time, don't expect too much of them—nor of folks neither. Not like this young gennulman," he added, casting a resentful glance at John. Then he looked searchingly at Charlotte. "You'm an Endacott, bain't 'ee, ma'am."

"Yes. My grandfather—" she began eagerly.

"Charlotte!" John tugged at her arm.

"I'm sorry. You have work to do, of course." Reluctantly she bade the old shepherd goodbye. "Perhaps I may meet you again."

" 'Tis more than likely. I don't move far afield—only up to the hills and back."

"What a narrow life that must be," John declared, hurrying Charlotte on towards the village.

"He seems contented enough."

"Naturally. He's old, his days are almost over."

"He was not always old," Charlotte pointed out. "But

he has always been a shepherd and wanted nothing more, it seems."

John shrugged. "Each man to his fancy. 'Tis not my idea of how to spend one's life."

"Yet I think it cannot easily be bettered. To know contentment and peace of mind is surely given to very few men. It is what Gervase is constantly seeking." She smiled, recalling the old man's words. "It is difficult to imagine Gervase as a shepherd, though. One can scarce visualise those elegant silk breeches and velevet coat amongst the sheep pens. Why, he even insisted on changing his suit when he had been thrown on to the gravel of the terrace at Stokeleigh. I will tell you about that now if you . . ."

But she saw that John was not even listening. He was staring, with narrowed eyes, at a piece of level ground on which geese were grazing.

"That is where I would recommend the new cottages to be built," he said with conviction. "I will take some measurements while we are waiting for Endacott."

"Can I be of any help to you?" Charlotte asked.

John shook his head.

"Then I will walk over to the river and gather some of the flowers that are growing there," Charlotte said.

He nodded absentmindedly, already absorbed in his calculations.

As she made her way over the rough grass, Charlotte felt a little prick of resentment. She had been anxious to confide in John, to hear him side with her as she was sure he would do. And she was disappointed that the flock of sheep had cut short what he had been about to say in the lane. He had spoken of the future of America, of his own plans, and asked her if she did not look forward to a part in them. Was it not justifiable then, to suppose his next words would have concerned their marriage?

How would she have answered? Accepted him at once? Or dissembled a little, not seeming too eager? She glanced back to where he was pacing out the land, utterly absorbed in his task. A man of ambition, a man in a hurry, as the shepherd had been quick to realise. Not like Gervase . . .

She saw Gervase coming along the lane, still walking a little stiffly. He wore a green broadcloth coat which merged with the landscape. His fair hair gleamed in the sunlight. He sat down on a fallen branch and waited for John to finish his calculations. When the younger man joined him, Charlotte heard him ask, "Where is Charlotte?"

John gestured vaguely towards the river, then sat beside Gervase, his drawing-board on his knee. He was evidently outlining his plans, with quick stabs of his finger on the board, and expressive waves of his hand towards the ground he had selected. Gervase crossed one leg over the other and listened to John without interrupting, thoughtfully rubbing his cheek.

Charlotte continued towards the river, and sat on the bank. Unexpectedly, the loneliness she had experienced in Exeter cathedral swept over her again. In a wave of dejection, she felt cut off, unwanted. All her life she had been loved and needed. For, even after her mother's death, Aunt Lucy had been glad of her help in return for giving her a home. Now, it seemed, she could help no one, not even John. There was no real place for her at Stokeleigh. And as for Gervase . . .

She leaned forward to pick some of the wild flowers growing on the bank. It was then she saw the child: a girl about five years old, peering at her from behind a low bush.

Charlotte held out her hand. "Come and smell my flowers. Are they not pretty?"

The child emerged from her hiding-place and advanced cautiously, fingers in mouth. She had a halo of fair curls. Her cheeks were healthily pink and her blue dress, though torn, was tolerably clean.

As she hesitated, Charlotte beckoned. "Come along,

do not be afraid. It is a long time since I talked to a little girl like you."

The child moved forward again, not taking her blue eyes from Charlotte's face. When she was close enough, Charlotte broke off a spray of blossom.

"There, we will tuck it into your dress. Now you are like a grand lady, with a flower in your gown."

The little girl giggled, and flopped down beside Charlotte. Copying her companion, she broke off another spray and pushed the stem through a buttonhole of Charlotte's bodice.

Charlotte laughed delightedly. "What is your name?"

The child mumbled something unintelligible.

"Say it again," Charlotte urged. "I come from a different land, over the sea, and it is not easy for me to understand what you say. Tell me again, slowly."

"My name is Lucy Thomson."

"Lucy? Oh, I like that name. I have an aunt called Lucy."

"Where does she live?" the child asked.

"A long way away, in America."

"What's *your* name?"

"Charlotte. Charlotte Endacott."

The child regarded her solemnly, then pointed towards Stokeleigh. "From up there?"

"Yes, from up there. And where do you live?"

Lucy pointed again, this time towards the row of cottages beside the river.

"Shall we pick some more flowers?" she suggested.

Together they picked a big bunch. Then Charlotte found some slivers of wood and fixed leaves in them as sails. They took one each, and, leaning over the bank, put them in the water, and, at a word from Charlotte, let them go simultaneously. When the little craft were out of sight, the child turned to her, cheeks flushed, eyes bright.

"Again. Again. Can we have another race?"

Charlotte fashioned more boats, and soon they learned

where the water ran more swiftly. Lucy grew so excited that Charlotte kept firm hold of her skirts to stop her falling in. They were so absorbed in their game that a woman's voice calling from along the river path, startled them both.

Lucy looked up. "That's Mam, coming to fetch me."

A young woman was approaching them. She was dressed in blue, like her child, with a clean apron over her gown and a white cap on her brown hair. She had a pleasant, open face, and it was a few moments before Charlotte recognised her as one of the women who had confronted John so angrily.

"Lucy, you'm not to bother the lady," she admonished.

Smiling, Charlotte said, "She's no bother. She's very sweet."

The little girl edged nearer to Charlotte. "The lady gived me flowers and I gived her some, and then she made some boats and we raced un and I've winned nearly ever time."

The young woman appeared confused. " 'Twas very kind of you, ma'am, to take such an interest, especially after what happened t'other day. I'd like to say I be mortal sorry for the way we behaved. Us didn't give the gennulman who was with 'ee time to explain when 'e said the cottages was to come down . . ."

"You were afraid your homes were to be taken from you?" Charlotte helped her out. "But Mr. Endacott planned to provide you with other, better cottages. You know that now, I think."

The woman nodded. " 'Tis on account of us allus thinking 'e be like 'is father, you see. The old master'd not a mite o' kindness in him, tho' I s'pose I shouldn't say such a thing to you, ma'am."

Lucy jumped to her feet. "Have 'ee made the oatcakes, Mam? Can I have one? Then can I go on playing?"

The young woman shook the child's arm. "Doan' 'ee be so rude. Whatever will Miss Endacott think of 'ee?"

Charlotte rose and brushed the bits of twig and

leaves from her skirt. "I think I had better join . . ." But, glancing towards the level stretch of ground, she saw that the men were standing with their backs to her, deep in consultation. She sighed and turned back to the woman. "It seems they have forgotten me," she said, smiling ruefully.

Mrs. Thomson screwed up her apron with workworn fingers and cleared her throat nervously. "If so be you'd care for a cup of goat's milk, ma'am, and a taste of my oatcakes . . ."

"How kind of you," Charlotte said at once. "I should like that very much."

The woman flushed with pleasure, "I was a bit afeared to ask 'ee. It wasn't the late Mistress Endacott's way to visit in the village, and Miss Pendleton is allus too busy to do more than bid us good-day. But I'd be glad to welcome you to my cottage, though 'tis only a small place as you must know."

The child put her hand in Charlotte's as they went along the path. Charlotte found it difficult to understand all that Lucy said, but her mother's speech was not so broad. The cottage was tiny, sparsely furnished, but gay with rugs and cheap coloured china. An iron kettle sang on the hob; the fire was banked up with turves. Mrs. Thomson pulled forward a wheelback chair, dusting it carefully with her apron.

Charlotte sat down, the child pressing against her. Through the open door she could see the river, only a few yards away.

"Taken a proper fancy to you, ma'am, has Lucy," Mrs. Thomson remarked, setting a blue and white cup and plate on the table.

Charlotte put her arm around the little girl. "I am fond of children, and quite used to them. I helped my mother teach school." She broke off at the look of astonishment on the young woman's face. "That was after my father died," she went on to explain. "We were quite poor then."

Mrs. Thomson said incredulously, "But you'm an Endacott, ma'am. The Endacotts be rich folk, allus have been."

"In England, perhaps. In the part of America where I lived, life is much harder, except for a very few." Seeing the woman still looking doubtful, she tried to make it clearer. "I know it may be difficult for you to understand, and even Mr. Endacott does not quite believe me, I think. But my home in Southport was little bigger than your cottage until my father built on other rooms. And it was made of wood, not stone."

Mrs. Thomson shook her head, apparently unconvinced. The child, gazing up at Charlotte with her big blue eyes, said, "You were singing as you made the boats. Sing again, now."

"Lucy!" Her mother's voice was sharp with protest. "You must not speak to Miss Endacott like that."

Seeing the hurt look on the little girl's face, Charlotte said at once, "I do not mind, Mrs. Thomson. It was a song my nurse taught me. It goes like this."

She began to hum, then paused. "Try it after me."

Lucy did her best, while her mother looked on in amazement. Charlotte lifted the child on to her lap. "Now, try again, like this."

A shadow fell across the sunlit doorway, the view of the river was blocked by a man's figure. It took Charlotte a moment or two, looking against the light, to recognise Gervase.

The woman hastily put down the jug from which she had been pouring goat's milk. "Be you looking for Miss Endacott, zur? I hope I didn't do wrong, but . . ."

Charlotte cut short the woman's nervous explanation. "Mrs. Thomson invited me in to sample her oatcakes."

"That was kind," Gervase said, stooping under the low lintel. "May I do the same?"

"Certainly, zur, you'm welcome," the young woman answered, and went to fetch more milk.

Gervase said, "Mr. Standish did not seem to know

where you had gone, Charlotte, so I came in search of you. He said you went towards the river, and when I could not see you, I—I became worried."

"You thought I had fallen in?" she asked in astonishment. "Gervase, that was foolish."

"Yes." He bent his head and fingered his shirt cuff. "But you know my feelings about the river." He turned to Mrs. Thomson. "I want to have you all moved from here as soon as possible. The river looks harmless enough at present, but you know well enough how quickly it can rise when there has been heavy rain in the hills."

"There be talk of Sir William Ransom altering the course of the river on 'is land, zur. Is it true?"

"The work was started this morning, I am informed. That is why Mr. Standish is over on the green drawing up plans for the new cottages."

Mrs. Thomson, handing round a plate of oatcakes, glanced out the door. "I mind the time the water came right through the cottage. A foot high it were, and everything covered with mud afterwards. It took us women a week of scrubbing to get the places clean."

"I can well believe it. You have been told, I hope, that the new cottages will be bigger and more convenient?"

"Yes, zur, indeed. Some of the older women doan't want to move. 'Tis a case of what was good enough for their mothers being good enough for them. But I'll be glad to, myself." Self-consciously she smoothed her apron. "With another one on the way, we'm a bit cramped here. And I've never taken to the sound of the river at night, so close it seems in the quiet. Is our rent to be raised, zur, when the new cottages be built?"

Gervase smiled and put down his cup. "If it is, Mrs. Thomson, you may rest assured your husband's wages will be increased to meet it."

"Thank 'ee, zur, I'll tell my man that. Matt the shepherd told us that if we bided our time, things would be different when you were maister. Now us knows to trust 'ee, and with Miss Endacott at Stokeleigh, too, things will be much better, I can see. I heard tell 'twas her that stopped Sir William attacking our men on Saturday, and bound up my brother-in-law's wrist. But there, zur, I dare say you doan't want to be reminded of that. 'Twas a daft thing they men did, going up to Stokeleigh with scythes and pitchforks and such. Some of us think 'twould have served them right if Sir William's servants *had* laid into them."

"You are wrong," Gervase said, biting into a second oatcake. "It would have led to a violent and useless fight, and solved no problems at all. It was entirely thanks to Miss Endacott that the situation was saved."

Charlotte gasped. "You say that? And yet . . ." She broke off in confusion as she became aware of Mrs. Thomson's interested gaze.

She put Lucy gently from her lap and rose. "Thank you, Mrs. Thomson. Your cakes were delicious and the milk most refreshing."

"Will you come again?" Lucy demanded. "And teach me that song?"

"Perhaps," Charlotte answered and bent to kiss the child.

Outside, Gervase said, "That song you were teaching the child, and the one you hummed as you mended my coat—they sounded so sad. I do not remember hearing them before."

"They are songs Bella taught me, songs which are sung by the slaves on the plantations in the south. Mostly they are sad, expressing a longing for their own country."

"Is that why *you* sing them?" His tone was bitter. "I suppose you count the days until the time when you will sail with John Standish, back to America, vowing never to set foot in England again."

She was silent for a few moments. Then she answered thoughtfully, "Earlier today I would have answered without hesitation, for England has shown me little that I admire or wish for. Now . . . It sounds foolish, but I met an old shepherd in the lane and he spoke of things I understood. And just now, when the child came to me and we played together, and then Mrs. Thomson took me into her cottage . . ." She laughed shortly. "That would seem to prove, would it not, that I am more at home with people who live close to the earth, who have to make their way in the world? It is what I have tried to tell you, more than once."

"And the rest of us have nothing to offer you? Even I, of your own family . . ."

"You may be of my family, but we are worlds apart. I have told you that too, Gervase. What happened on Saturday proved it. To me it was natural to behave as I did. To you, it was an embarrassment."

"Oh, Charlotte. Charlotte. If only you understood." He turned away from her and stood staring down into the water, his hands clenched, his face so pale and strained that she was suddenly anxious.

"What is the matter, Gervase? Are you ill?"

"Leave me, Charlotte." His words were scarcely audible.

Charlotte hesitated, at a loss. Gervase made a dismissive gesture. And so, perplexed, she went to seek John and found him, sitting on the fallen branch, happily absorbed in his drawings. He greeted her with a smile and made room for her beside him. She sat down and watched as the plans for the new cottages took shape under his skilled fingers.

"They will have that slope as protection from the north," he explained, pointing it out to her. "There will be stairs here, and two rooms above. Endacott tells me the present cottages have nothing but a rickety landing leading to a trapdoor, and no window on the upper floor at all."

"Is he pleased with your plans?" Charlotte asked.

"Yes, indeed. He will put them into practice straight away. He even talks of ordering material at once."

"I thought the idea was to utilise the stone from the old cottages."

"That was my idea. But Endacott has no need to economise in such a way. He is all for the work being put in hand immediately."

"Because of some alterations his neighbour is making, it appears."

John shuffled his papers together and rose, stretching out a hand to help her up. "I think he is making a great deal too much fuss over it. I cannot see that it will increase the danger of flooding in the least, and I think I am likely to know more about it than Endacott."

She looked up at him, seeing the familiar thrust of his chin, the firm line of his mouth, the bold eyes full of assurance. And, suddenly, she had an odd desire to prick the bubble of his self-confidence, for she saw that, in his own way, he could be as arrogant as she had thought Gervase.

She said stubbornly, "I would have thought that Gervase, who has lived here all his life and knows the vagaries of the river, would be the better judge of what may happen."

John glanced at her in surprise. "You change as quickly as the English weather, Charlotte. Not two hours since, you had not a good word to say for your guardian. Yet now you take his side."

"I am not taking his side," she protested. "I am just trying to be fair."

John laughed shortly. "That is something women never are. They are much too prone to be swayed by emotion."

She faced him, the colour flooding into her cheeks. "You cannot suppose that to be so in this case?"

"Indeed I hope not. For I have already told you, Charlotte, that I will not play second-fiddle. Nor will I have my judgments questioned." He drew her hand through his arm. "Come, let us go along the lane where we may talk without an audience of curious villagers."

In silence they walked between the cottages to the further side of the village. Charlotte caught sight of Gervase, talking to a group of women who were spreading their washing on the river bank. She heard them laugh at some remark of his. Then John was speaking again.

"I have been considering, Charlotte, where we should set up house. I think it should be Boston, for that town is likely to be the centre of the movement for independence. And by the time our children are old enough to attend, the schooling should be excellent."

She was taken aback. He had not even mentioned marriage, yet he was calmly speaking of a home and children as if the matter was already settled. Where was any declaration of love, or the desire to kiss her he had expressed when they walked along the river path? She felt the same chill she had experienced when, realising he had forgotten her presence, she had left him to his work.

He stopped and pulled her round to face him. "You are not listening, Charlotte."

"I—I am surprised," she stammered. "You speak so definitely of 'we' and 'our.' "

"Naturally. I think I have made it plain that I wish you to share my future. And I cannot but suppose, from your attitude towards me, that you are of the same mind. I think that we should be married in England, so that I can offer you the greater protection on the journey home. Do you not agree?"

Charlotte swallowed hard and tried to answer lightly, happily. After all, was he not offering her everything she longed for?"

"Oh yes, it would seem quite the best plan."

As if reading her thoughts, John took her hands in his. "Forgive me, you must think me a casual fellow. But, to tell the truth, when I am at work I become so absorbed it is difficult for my thoughts to be distracted by other matters. But to you, naturally, the question of marriage is of the greatest importance." He drew her towards him, smiling down at her. "I will be good to you, Charlotte, never fear. And now that we are betrothed, may I be allowed to kiss you?"

She tilted up her face and closed her eyes. She expected to feel herself soaring away on a cloud, for that was what Aunt Lucy had assured her would happen when she fell in love. But, to her dismay, her feet and her thoughts stayed firmly on the ground.

John released her. "There now, it is settled. You are happy, Charlotte?"

"Oh yes, very happy."

She hoped her words sounded more convincing to John than they did to herself. In a kind of panic, she tried to fathom what had happened to her. If John had spoken like this, kissed her like this, three days ago upon the river path, she would have felt so differently, been so truly, wonderfully happy. Could it be that a proposal of marriage was never as delightful and as thrilling as one expected? Was the anticipation of the first kiss so much pleasanter than the reality?

She took herself to task, telling herself she was the most fortunate woman in the world, that the future stretched bright and exciting before her. She matched her step to John's and held tightly to his arm as they made their way up the drive to Stokeleigh.

Thomas came along the terrace to meet them. "Is the master not with you, ma'am?" he asked, his forehead creased with anxiety.

"He is still down at the village, I think. Why, what has happened?"

" 'Tis Miss Pendleton, ma'am."

"Rebecca, you mean? Has something happened to her?" Charlotte freed herself from John's arm. "I will go in at once."

The footman stepped in front of her. "No, ma'am, 'tis Miss Sophia Pendleton I'm speaking of. She's here, ma'-

am, rode through the woods and across the little bridge further down river."

"Then you had better tell her that Mr. Endacott will be along shortly."

"Yes, ma'am, I'll do that." Thomas did not move, but stood on one foot, then the other, scratching his forehead beneath his wig.

"What is the matter?" Charlotte asked. "You are not usually so slow."

He rubbed his hands down his breeches. "The fact is, ma'am, I've seen Miss Pendleton in some proper rages. But I bain't never seen her in quite such a tear as she be now. I reckon you'd best keep out of her way, ma'am, until the master comes."

Sophia refused to sit down. She stood in the middle of the drawing-room, her cheeks almost the colour of her crimson riding habit, her eyes glittering. Her cravat looked too tight; the ostrich feather sweeping down from her hat quivered.

It occurred to Charlotte, sitting beside Gervase on the sofa, that there was a certain similarity between Sophia and Sir William Ransom. Both of them dressed in flamboyant clothes, and were loud-voiced and excitable. Like Sir William, Sophia gave vent to the mood of the moment and too often, it seemed to Charlotte, that mood was one of anger.

"I have forgiven you many things, Gervase," Sophia declared, as she paced across the room. "This time you have gone too far. That you could allow this girl to take the part of a pack of common labourers against a neighbour who had come to your aid—it is too much! And to permit her to attack Sir William, for all the world like a common fishwife . . ." She broke off and laughed scornfully. "That is an appropriate description, is it not? For I understand her father was no more than an ordinary fisherman." Imperiously she raised a hand as Gervase was about to protest. "Wait, I have by no means finished." She ran the thong of her whip through her fingers. "How you could tolerate such an exhibition is beyond my comprehension. To stand there, and . . ."

"In actual fact, I was on the gravel, pinned down by Ransom's legs," Gervase interrupted calmly, and, despite herself, Charlotte was tempted to laugh.

Sophia glared at him. "And how, may I ask, did you come to be there, except by being knocked down by one of those ignorant brutes from the village? But for Will . . ."

"But for Ransom, the matter would have ended peaceably, with neither hurt nor loss of dignity on either side. Instead, the blundering fool came galloping up the drive, shouting and hallooing as if he were riding across country after a fox. Since he would not listen to reason, Charlotte very bravely took it upon herself . . ."

"*Bravely?* You really expect me to stay here and listen to such lies, such arrant nonsense?"

Gervase rose and went to her. His voice was quiet. "You may stay or go as you wish, Sophia. But one thing you will understand. You will offer no more insults to Charlotte. She acted in the way she thought best to help me, and in the interests of what I strongly believe in, justice. Ransom has his own way of administering what he calls justice—with a whip or a cudgel, or committal to gaol without a trial. It is not my way, and never will be."

"He is worth twenty of you."

"Possibly," Gervase said drily. "Just as, in your opinion, Henry was worth twenty of me. Unfortunately for you, Sophia, you have to make do with me. And it is time you accepted the fact that I shall not change. Doubtless Henry would have dealt with your tantrums by putting you across his knee and administering a sound spanking, and you would have felt the better for it. Though I have no intention of treating you like that, there are certain limits to which I will not allow you to go."

"Such as?" she demanded, with an insolent jerk of the head which reminded Charlotte of Rebecca.

"You are well aware to what I am referring."

"If you think I will give him up . . ."

Charlotte rose and made quietly for the door. Sophia strode across the room to bar her way.

"I have not finished with *you* yet." She turned back to Gervase. "Do you suppose I will accept threats from you while you fall over backwards to excuse this chit's behaviour?"

Gervase moved swiftly. "Stand away from that door," he ordered, and his voice had an unfamiliar edge on it.

Sophia stood her ground, her chin thrust up. The velvet of her habit was stretched tightly across her chest.

"And if I do not?"

Gervase looked straight into her eyes. "You will find yourself another husband, Sophia. And you are twenty-four."

With a startled exclamation, she drew back, staring at him as if she could believe neither eyes nor ears.

"How could you? How *could* you be so cruel?"

Gervase shrugged. "You have only yourself to blame. I gave you due warning."

A moment longer Sophia stood there, the colour fading from her cheeks, her eyes no longer bold. Then she caught up her gloves from a side table, and turning on her heel, swept out of the room and across the hall. A few minutes later she rode past the window in a flash of crimson and a flurry of gravel, at her heels a red-faced groom trying to get his foot into a dangling stirrup.

Charlotte, avoiding Gervase's eyes, asked, "May I go now?"

He moved from beside the door. As she passed him, he put out a hand.

"Charlotte, I am sorry you were witness to such a scene. I lost my temper. It does not happen often. But I have rarely been so angry. Do you think very badly of me for what I said to Sophia?"

"It is not for me to think well or ill of how you treat your future wife, Gervase. It is quite obvious that neither of you has the least affection for the other."

"You must know by now where Sophia's affections lie."

"With Sir William Ransom?" she asked, suddenly seeing the truth and surprised she had not realised it before.

Gervase nodded. "He is very like my brother Henry."

"And you tolerate the situation?"

"What else can I do? It gives Sophia some measure of solace, of happiness. It does his wife no harm, for, as I told you, he remains as devoted to her as a man can be to a constant invalid. But after Sophia and I have married . . ." He broke off and passed a hand wearily across his forehead. "If only she had accepted my threat and thought fit to end our betrothal."

"Cannot you do so, if it is so very irksome to you?"

He looked at her in surprise. "*I* end it? There is a legal contract, Charlotte."

She laughed shortly. "So it is in order for Sophia to break the contract, but not for you?"

"Naturally. She is a woman and can change her mind. As a man of honour, I am bound by my word."

She shook her head in perplexity. "I'm at a loss to understand these separate codes of behaviour. Once *my* word was given, I would feel bound by it as much as any man."

Gervase walked slowly over to the fireplace and stood in silence, his back towards her. When he spoke, it was in the same strained voice which had so puzzled her as they parted by the river.

"And have you given your word, Charlotte? Have you given a promise which you will never break?"

For a moment she hesitated, troubled by a strange reluctance to answer him. Then she said firmly. "Yes, Gervase, I have. I became betrothed to John Standish an hour ago."

Rebecca, dressed in cloak and bonnet, came to the door of Charlotte's room.

"Was that Sophia galloping so madly down the drive?"

"Yes."

"There were two horses, I thought. Did our groom go with her?"

"Yes," Charlotte said again, not wishing to be involved in an explanation.

The girl pulled off her bonnet. "There are times when I think my sister to be quite beyond understanding. She bade me to be absolutely ready to accompany her home. She expected me to ride pillion behind Tobias when she knew perfectly well that I brought only carriage clothes with me. And now she rides off, I suppose in a great tear with Gervase as usual, and leaves me stranded." She gave an exaggerated shrug. "Not that I mind. This house of late has been vastly more entertaining than home, especially when Papa is ailing and one has to creep around like a mouse."

Suddenly she dropped her grown-up air and became an inquisitive child. "Was she very angry with Gervase? And with you, for pummelling Sir William like that?" She giggled. "I should dearly love to have seen you. I think he is a stupid oaf, and how Sophia can prefer him to Gervase is beyond my comprehension. Do you not agree, ma'am?"

Charlotte answered guardedly. "We do not all admire the same type of man, Rebecca. Indeed, it would work out badly if we did."

"But you admire Gervase, do you not?" As Charlotte crossed to her little dressing-table, the girl followed her and spoke to Charlotte's image in the mirror. "You admire him very much, don't you? Oh, you try to hide it, but I can see."

Charlotte met the girl's gaze in the mirror. Instead of replying to the question, she said evenly, "I have some news which may interest you, Rebecca. This afternoon I accepted Mr. Standish's offer of marriage."

The girl's lips parted, her eyes widened. "But I thought . . ." As Charlotte turned away, Rebecca caught at her arm. "You are really set on leaving Stokeleigh? On leaving Gervase and going back to America?"

"Certainly. I am assured it will please everybody as well as myself. As far as Gervase is concerned, it will make his life a great deal easier, for which he will doubtless be very thankful."

The girl stared into Charlotte's eyes. "Is that what you truly think?" she demanded in a tone of the utmost disbelief. "Are you so blind?"

"Rebecca, I do not know what you are talking about," Charlotte said sharply. "And I should be obliged if you would leave me now, since I wish to change my gown."

Reluctantly the girl walked to the door, then turned. "If Gervase ever looked at me the way he looks at you . . ." She broke off as Charlotte opened a drawer, and asked in surprise, "Is that a doll you have there?"

"Yes. It is a puppet worked by strings."

"I would not have thought you would play with a doll, ma'am."

Charlotte searched for a pair of stockings. "I had it given to me—by mistake. This afternoon I made friends with one of the children from the cottages by the river. It is my intention to give the doll to her the next time I go down to the village."

Rebecca came forward and examined the gay plaything. "It is too good for a labourer's child. Who gave it to you? Mr. Standish?"

Charlotte almost snatched the puppet from Rebecca's hands. "No, not Mr. Standish. Someone who—who did not know my age."

The girl said impatiently. "You are talking in riddles Do you mean that it was sent to you by an aunt or some other relative, who . . . ?"

Charlotte set the doll down firmly upon a chair. "Rebecca, I am not prepared to answer any more questions. You will be good enough to do as I asked, and leave me now. And you had better take off your cloak, since it seems unlikely that your sister will return for you."

When the door closed behind the girl, Charlotte stood looking down at the Spanish doll Gervase had given her. She could remember every detail of that scene on board ship when he had pulled the puppet from his pocket and thrust it into her unwilling hands.

"I bought this for the child," he had said, "though I am not sure of her age."

He had bought it for the child he had thought Charlotte Endacott to be. She could picture him, in his elegant suit and gold-trimmed tricorne pointing with his cane to the toy he had selected, producing his purse and paying for the doll in his languid, superior way.

But was that picture the true one? She had so many different ones now. Gervase, venturing alone into the night to face the man he thought had come to take his life; unarmed on the terrace, confronting the villagers as they brandished their primitive weapons. Gervase, tumbled in the dust at Tiverton but concerned for her safety; taking her part against Sophia, Rebecca and Sir William Ransom; standing dejectedly beside the river as he said, "Oh, Charlotte, if only you understood." And just now, when she had told him of her betrothal, he had winced as if she had struck him, and his voice had been oddly muffled as he wished her every happiness.

She picked up the doll and automatically pulled the strings.

"Keep it for your first-born daughter," he had told her. Her daughter. And John's?

She experienced again the sense of panic which had seized her in the lane. She felt trapped, as helpless as the puppet whose arms and legs could be jerked this way and that. But the puppet had no heart, no feelings. And it was her own emotions over which Charlotte seemed to have lost control.

While she dressed for supper, her mind sought for

a means of escape from Stokeleigh, the house which seemed never to have known love or happiness, and from its owner, whose change of heart was making it even more impossible for her to stay.

IX

Charlotte folded her napkin and rose from the breakfast table. "Will you go up to the schoolroom, Rebecca? I wish to speak to Gervase."

The girl gave her a calculating look, but went without protest. Gervase looked troubled.

"You are under no obligation to continue these lessons, Charlotte."

"I quite enjoy them," she told him. "Rebecca is a very apt pupil."

"It sounds so strange to hear you use that word."

"It is not strange in the least. As I told you, I helped my mother teach school."

"You could have been scarcely more than a child yourself."

"I was fifteen."

He looked at her thoughtfully. "There are times when you seem little older than that now, when you seem so young and—and defenceless. Yet, at others, I could believe you older and wiser than myself."

She laughed. "In truth, you were not very wise yesterday in your attitude to Sophia. I fear she will make you pay for that."

"She will make me pay for something or other for the rest of my life," he said ruefully. "Yet, riled as I may be, I shall feel pity for her since, in her estimation, I shall so often fail her."

Charlotte clasped her fingers together. "Gervase, I have two requests to make of you."

Smiling, he spoke in his former debonair manner. "They are granted already."

She avoided his eyes. "I would like to go into Tiverton and wondered if you would be kind enough to loan me the mare, and allow Thomas to accompany me."

"I will do better than that," he said at once. "I myself will accompany you. I had planned to go into the town today and see several merchants about building materials, and arrange for the hire of some labourers for the work on the cottages."

Disconcerted, Charlotte said hesitantly, "I would not wish to waste your time."

He looked searchingly into her face. "Is my company so irksome to you, Charlotte?"

"No. No, of course not." Annoyed to feel the colour rushing to her cheeks, she added hastily, "It is just that I want—that is, there are several matters I wish to attend to."

"In fact, you wish to visit John Standish? Is that it?" As, still not looking at him, she nodded, he said, "I envy him, that you should be so eager for his company."

"Oh, it is not that at all. It is . . ." She broke off in confusion, since it was impossible to explain her real reason for wishing to consult John.

"And the other request?" Gervase prompted gently.

Charlotte picked up a fork and absentmindedly ran the prongs along the table cloth. "I wondered, since Great-uncle Matthew had offered to provide a home for me, whether . . . You have been most generous in your hospitality, Gervase, and I am grateful. But the fact is . . ."

"That you wish to make some purchases and are without money? Forgive me, I have been very thoughtless." He took his purse from his coat pocket and emptied it on the table. There, take all of it. I can visit the bank in Tiverton."

As, not without embarrassment, she gathered up the coins, he said reluctantly, "Doubtless you would prefer

Standish to accompany you when you make your purchases. But at least you must allow me to escort you to Tiverton, Charlotte. I am assured there will be no repetition of the unfortunate incident that occurred on our previous visit. I have learned that I am no longer regarded with such hostility. It has been accepted that Biddlecombe died from falling over the bridge, and word has reached Tiverton of what I propose to do for the cottagers."

"I am glad of that, Gervase. It was so unfair, the way those men treated you."

He rubbed his cheek. "Men's attitudes alter in the oddest way. That firebrand Joshua Batten, who is a mason and has, of course, been unable to work on account of the injury to his wrist—for which I am paying him compensation above what he will receive from his club—is now my loudest advocate. And you, Charlotte, will be shown the utmost respect by the people who formerly threatened you."

On that occasion, she recalled, John had taken her to his lodgings as a means of escape from the unruly mob. This time she was going there for the same reason—to seek escape. But not from physical danger. She was running away from an intolerable situation. And from something more, a small inner voice insisted. Some truth she did not want to recognise. For if she did, she would never again know a moment's peace of mind.

"Why cannot I come with you?" Rebecca demanded, when Charlotte told her of the outing to Tiverton.

"For one thing, you told me only yesterday that you have no riding clothes with you."

"We could go in Gervase's carriage."

"That would not be convenient, since Gervase and I are going our own ways in the town."

"I could ride pillion behind Thomas."

"Thomas is not coming with us."

The girl pouted. "The truth is, you do not want me, either of you."

Charlotte said quietly, "You are right, Rebecca. I am visiting Mr. Standish to discuss some—some matters concerning our future. And Gervase will be calling upon various merchants."

"Oh, very well." The girl tossed her head. "In any case, I think it is going to rain. My chest hurts. There is so little air this morning; there will be a thunderstorm before the day is out."

Charlotte glanced out of the schoolroom window. The sky was leaden. Not a leaf stirred.

"Do you not think it is likely your sister will come for you today?"

Rebecca shrugged. "How should I know?" She glanced up at Charlotte. "Does Sophia know you are betrothed to Mr. Standish?"

"No. She left before I had even told Gervase."

"The news will doubtless please her. It does not please me."

"Why ever not?"

The girl replied truculently, "Because you could have done what Sophia will never do."

"What is that?"

"Make Gervase happy." The words were forced out. Rebecca rose and stood with her hands on the desk, leaning across it. "You are so full of thoughts of America, you cannot see what is under your nose. You have not even noticed, I suppose, that I am in love with Gervase." Ignoring Charlotte's startled exclamation, she went on in a rush, "I have loved him since I was a little girl and he gave me piggy-backs—properly, not like that clumsy Henry, who banged my head on the beams. I used to think of Gervase as a kind of hero, like the knights in the story-books—the gentle ones who fought only in defence of their honour, or a lady. It's different now. I'm old enough, though you do not think so, to love him as he really is. But, like you, he still thinks of me as a child, and always will. So . . ." She broke off, covering her face with her hands. Her thin shoulders shook as the sobs rasped in her throat.

Charlotte was round the desk in a moment. "Becky, my poor child. I did not know you felt like this."

The girl exclaimed bitterly. "There, you see! I am only a child in your eyes."

"I am sorry. I said it without thinking. Sit down, dear, and stop crying. You will make yourself cough."

To Charlotte's surprise, Rebecca did as she was bid. She made no attempt to push away Charlotte's arm. Instead she leaned against her and caught hold of her hand.

"Don't go away," she pleaded tearfully. "Don't go to America. Gervase will be so unhappy."

"But, Becky, I must go. I have given my promise to Mr. Standish. In any case, Gervase is betrothed to your sister."

"Sophia has Sir William Ransom," the girl argued stubbornly. "And Mr. Standish could find someone else. For 'tis obvious he is not head over heels in love with you. But Gervase . . ."

"What about Gervase?" His voice startled them both. "Why, what is the matter with Becky?" he asked, hesitating in the doorway.

"She is not feeling well," Charlotte answered quickly. "It is very close this morning and her chest is hurting. I think she should lie down for a while. I will stay with her."

"But you wanted to go into Tiverton," Gervase pointed out.

Charlotte shook her head. "It is not that important. You had best go alone. My—my shopping can wait."

He came further into the room, peering anxiously at Rebecca's flushed and tearstained face. "Do you think we should send for Sophia?"

"No. *No!*" The girl almost shouted her refusal. "I do

not want Sophia. Charlotte is being very kind. I would rather be with her."

Gervase raised his eyebrows and shrugged helplessly. "I suppose I never shall understand the female mind. I thought you two to be at loggerheads."

"Not any longer," Charlotte said. "Leave us, if you please, Gervase. I will take Rebecca to her room."

As she put her arm around the girl's shoulders, Charlotte realised how thin she was. In the bedroom, Rebecca was seized with a fit of coughing. When it subsided, she said breathlessly, "You need not stay with me, if you are anxious to go to . . ."

"I shall stay. Do you not think you should lie down? I will prop you up with these pillows."

Obediently Rebecca got on the bed and allowed Charlotte to arrange the pillows and take off her shoes.

"I do not know why you are being so kind, after the way I have behaved to you," she said. "I have been quite horrid, have I not?"

Sitting on the bed, Charlotte took the girl's hand. "It does not matter, Becky. I did not know that you were unhappy and ill."

"But it doesn't make any difference, does it? You will still go away?"

"Yes, I will still go away. I have given my promise."

Rebecca jerked at Charlotte's hand. "But you don't love this American, do you? Not truly love him, as I love Gervase, so that his happiness matters above everything else in the whole world?"

Charlotte rose and went to the window. Rebecca's voice was triumphant.

"There, you see! You cannot answer me!"

"You should not ask such questions."

"Why not?" Again Rebecca started to cough.

Charlotte made for the door. "I am going downstairs to get you a drink. You are talking too much, it strains your chest."

From the kitchen window she saw Gervase mounting his horse in the stable yard. There was no spring in his step as there was in John's. He slouched in the saddle and held the reins loosely, as if it did not matter a whit whether his mount went left or right.

"Don't go away," Rebecca had pleaded. "Gervase will be so unhappy. You could make him happy."

She had been a fool to listen, Charlotte told herself. She should not have allowed the girl to put forward such an idea.

Mrs. Yeo bustled into the kitchen.

"Why, ma'am, you've let the milk boil over, and it's spilled on your gown. Let me wipe it down."

Charlotte stood submissively while the housekeeper cleaned her skirt; then sat on the hard kitchen chair while Mrs. Yeo heated another mugful of milk.

"I've heard you'm betrothed to the gentleman from America, ma'am," she remarked over her shoulder.

"Yes, that is so."

The housekeeper sniffed. "Then I'm sure I wish you happy. Though, from what you've said of the place, I should have thought you'd be glad not to go back. All them wild animals and savages and suchlike."

"We shall be living in a town, the biggest in Massachusetts."

"Indeed?"

It could have been the remotest village in Devon for all the impression it made on Mrs. Yeo. "Well, 'tis everyone to their own tastes, I suppose. 'Tis like we'll both be leaving Stokeleigh afore the year's out, I'm thinking."

"What do you mean?" asked Charlotte in surprise.

The housekeeper poured the steaming milk into a mug. "The moment Miss Pendleton steps in through the front door, out I goes through the back. That's what I mean, ma'am. I put up with a deal of trouble from the late Mrs. Endacott, but I was younger then and I'd not put anything away. Now I have, and I don't have to take orders from Miss Sophia or any other mistress I don't fancy. Shall I carry this upstairs for you?"

Charlotte rose. "Thank you, no. I am sure you have enough to do already." She hesitated, then asked, "Would you not be prepared to stay at Stokeleigh for Mr. Endacott's sake?"

The housekeeper smoothed her apron. "That's partly why I'd wish to go. I couldn't abide seeing his life made a proper misery by that—begging your pardon, ma'am, I shouldn't be talking like this to you. But I just about had enough of Miss Pendleton yesterday while she was waiting for Mr. Gervase to come back from the village. Poking here, prying there, running a finger over the furniture to see if she could find any dust, searching for cobwebs, even demanding the keys of my cupboards—for all the world as if she was mistress here already." She set a bowl on the table and emptied flour into it. "Of course," she added, as Charlotte was going out of the kitchen, "if 'twas someone like yourself as Mr. Gervase was marrying, 'twould be a very different kettle of fish. Always had a fancy to end my days at Stokeleigh. But 'tis a wish won't come true, I'm thinking."

Sitting beside Rebecca's bed, Charlotte added a soothing draught to the milk.

"Would you like me to read to you?" she asked.

"If you please."

Rebecca had again become the child she did not wish to be thought. After a while her eyelids drooped. Eventually, despite her efforts to keep awake, she dozed off.

Charlotte went downstairs and on to the terrace. The air was stifling. Her body felt clammy, her head as if there was a tight band around it. She was restless, yet without energy.

She heard a rumble of thunder in the distance. Momentarily the leaves stirred. Charlotte sat on the low balustrade, staring listlessly at the formal garden. A shower of rose petals fell on to her lap. Gervase had sat here, she recalled, the day he returned from Plymouth, the day she had been so angry with him.

She had never felt angry with John; only, at times, a little irritated. But then, neither had she felt sympathy for him, or pity, or any strong emotion. The feelings he aroused in her were respect, admiration, and a sense of ease in his company. She would be happy to go with him, in due course, back to their own country, and to escape from the difficulties she had met with in England.

She stood up abruptly, scattering the petals. Was that what he meant to her—a means of escape, just as Gervase had suggested? And if so, was that why, when he kissed her, she had remained entirely unmoved?

Despite the oppressive heat, she began to pace up and down the terrace. She was so absorbed in her thoughts that she did not hear a carriage approaching. When it appeared round the corner of the drive, she had to step quickly aside to avoid being run down. As the vehicle drew up before the front door, Charlotte recognised it as the Pendletons' carriage. Reluctantly she went forward as she realised the occupant had seen her.

"Gervase is not here," she told Sophia. "He has ridden into Tiverton."

The older woman, ignoring her footman's hand, stepped down. "I have come for Rebecca," she announced.

"I fear she is not well this morning, Miss Pendleton," Charlotte said. "Her chest was hurting and she was coughing, so I persuaded her to lie down. When I left her a short while since, she was asleep."

Sophia looked her up and down. "So you have elected to play nursemaid as well as governess? However, I do not intend to take your word. I shall go up and see for myself."

"As you wish."

Sophia asked insolently, "Will you not try to stop me?"

"Why should I?"

Sophia shrugged. "You appear to take so much upon yourself I would not have been surprised if you had attempted to bar my way."

Charlotte said with controlled anger, "I leave that practice to you, ma'am."

The older woman's eyes narrowed. She seemed about to make a biting retort, then changed her mind and went, with her usual determined step, into the house.

Five minutes later she reappeared.

"You are right," she conceded to Charlotte, who had seated herself again on the balustrade. "Rebecca is still asleep. Her appearance does not suggest that she has a fever. She is subject to these bouts of coughing, usually when the wind is cold."

"She told me she felt the lack of air. It is certainly very oppressive."

Sophia glanced at the sky. "We shall have a thunderstorm before long. I had best continue on my way to visit Lady Ransom with some calves' foot jelly my cook has prepared. I will call on my return and see how Rebecca is."

"I will tell her that," Charlotte said.

Sophia mounted the carriage steps. Looking down at Charlotte, she said casually, "Word has reached me that you have become betrothed to Mr. Standish. Is it true?"

"Quite true."

"I congratulate you. He appears to be an ambitious man and one with a great deal of talent. It would seem to be a good match; in fact, a better one than I myself could have arranged for you."

Again Charlotte controlled her anger. "I am gratified that you did not have to trouble yourself on my account, ma'am."

Sophia's eyes glinted. "When will you be married?"

"Later this year, before we sail for America."

Sophia smoothed her gloves. "I am pleased to hear it. For while you and Mr. Standish are busy putting America to rights, we shall be able to settle down here to our usual more tranquil existence."

As the carriage drew away, Charlotte's annoyance turned to amusement. The idea of Sophia Pendleton ever having led an existence which could be termed "tranquil" seemed so farcical that, despite the problems pressing upon her, Charlotte laughed aloud. Her laughter was drowned by another roll of thunder, nearer this time. She wondered if Gervase had reached Tiverton. The rain would come quite soon, she thought.

Deciding that it would be as well to take a little exercise before she was forced indoors, she went down the steps, along the path between the formal flower beds, and opened the little iron gate giving on to the river path. She turned to the right, away from the village. It was a direction she had not taken before and she trod cautiously, for the path was uneven and obstructed by the roots. The river looked dull as lead, almost black beneath the overhanging branches. In the field opposite, the cows were sluggishly flicking their tails against the troublesome flies. Swallows and martins skimmed low over the grass and the water. It was very still, the atmosphere heavy with the tension of the approaching storm.

Charlotte reverted to her former wariness, peering into the undergrowth, ears alert to every rustle, or snap of a twig. She tried to laugh off her fears, telling herself that the only real danger was from lightning when the storm came closer. But her nerves felt taut and stretched to their limit.

There was a strange, plopping sound on the water ahead of her; a figure emerged from behind a tree trunk. Bunching her skirts, Charlotte was about to turn tail and run, when she saw that what had alarmed her was merely a man fishing—a tall, slim man whose fair hair showed plainly against the dark bushes.

Gervase put down his rod and came towards her. "For the second time I have startled you. I am sorry."

"I thought you had gone to Tiverton."

"I started out, and then returned. Somehow I could not put my mind to bargaining with merchants. I would willingly have accompanied you, but when you changed your mind . . ."

She twisted her fingers together and said hesitantly, "I—I did not want you to come with me, Gervase. The plan I had in mind was better carried out without your knowledge."

"The plan?" he repeated in perplexity. "I thought your intention was to make some purchases."

"No." She bent her head and spoke very low. "My reason for going to Tiverton was to ask John to find me suitable lodgings in the town."

"*Charlotte!*" There was dismay in Gervase's voice.

A flash of lightning lit up the tops of the trees. They were both silent, waiting for the thunder. After it had passed, Gervase stepped closer to Charlotte.

"You were set on running away, is that it? But why, Charlotte? Have I not made it abundantly clear that you are welcome at Stokeleigh, that I want you."

Another rumble of thunder made him pause, so that the words "I want you" hung on the heavy, electrified air. They stared at one another. Charlotte's heart began to pound, and then to beat so loudly that it shut out the sound of thunder, of the river, everything save those words, "I want you."

Slowly Gervase raised his arms. "Charlotte, my dearest Charlotte."

Without the slightest hesitation, she went into his arms and laid her head on his chest and clung to him.

His lips caressed her hair, her temples, her neck. Then, as she lifted her face, he kissed her on the mouth. In that moment, she experienced all the feelings Aunt Lucy had described to her, and more. The world beyond his encircling arms was forgotten: the approaching storm; all the obstacles that lay between them; John,

Sophia. In all the world, there was only herself and Gervase.

They sat in the window embrasure in the library, holding hands, gazing despondently through the streaming panes at the grey sky; hearing the rain beat down on the gravel of the drive.

"What are we to do?" Gervase asked.

"What *can* we do? We are tied, both of us, by our promises." Charlotte laughed shortly. "Not that I did in fact give John a promise. For he did not ask me to marry him, in so many words. He took it for granted. I do not think that it even occurred to him that I might refuse, any more than he would doubt for a moment that he will succeed in all he attempts. But then, I suppose I made it only too obvious how much I wanted to escape, and to return to America."

"To escape from me?"

"Yes, and from Sophia's enmity, and a place where I felt I didn't belong. Now I see it was for another reason. It was because, although I tried to hide it, even from myself, I was falling in love with you. Oh, I have been so unfair to John. He is so kind, so thoughtful."

"Which I am not?"

She jerked at his hand. "I did not say that. Gervase, you must stop being so full of doubts, so quick to blame yourself and to feel guilty."

He murmured some words she could not catch. "What was that?"

He smiled wryly. "You put me in mind of what the lawyer told me Uncle Matthew said when he changed his will in my favour. Mr. Melhuish could not understand what the old man meant, but I could."

"What did he say?"

"Something about my setting out to absolve the sins of my fathers, and that while I was about it, I could absolve his as well."

"And you think you are called upon to do just that? With no one to help you."

He bowed his head. "If I had you . . ."

She took his face between her hands. "Why did this happen? I did not want to come to Stokeleigh. You did not want me here. Yet now . . . When I go, I shall leave my heart behind."

The library door opened. Rebecca came in, then stopped abruptly at sight of them.

"I'm sorry," she said quickly, and made as if to go.

"Becky, are you all right?" Charlotte asked anxiously. "Are you feeling better?"

"Yes, thank you." The girl's voice was clipped, almost abrupt. "The storm is getting closer, isn't it?"

"Yes. Are you afraid?"

Rebecca shook her head and retreated towards the door. "Not really. But it *is* a bad one. I—I didn't know Gervase was here. I'll go and talk to Mrs. Yeo."

Gervase stretched out his hand. "Becky, please do not . . ."

"You need not be anxious, Gervase. I swear I will not breathe a word to Sophia."

She went out, carefully closing the door behind her. Puzzled, Gervase looked at Charlotte.

"You two have become friends?"

"Oh, yes. We share a secret."

A vivid flash of lightning made Charlotte blink and draw back from the window. The crack of thunder which followed brought them both to their feet. The shutters rattled. The floor shook beneath their feet. It felt as if the world was being torn apart.

Rebecca ran back into the library, white-faced. "That was . . ."

Her words were drowned by the frenzied barking of the dogs, a horse's shrill whinny.

"I had better have a look round outside," Gervase said. "You two stay here, but keep away from the window."

Even as he spoke, there was another blinding flash

of lightning, another tremendous crack, and reverberation. Rebecca clung to Charlotte.

"The thunder is louder than any I've ever heard," she declared fearfully. "It sounds as if the whole house might fall down."

Gervase returned in a few minutes, his coat dark with rain.

"There does not appear to be any damage. Benedict is with the horses and Thomas is trying to quiet a maid who is having hysterics. The others have scuttled into dark cupboards. Even Mrs. Yeo interrupted her baking to offer up a quick prayer."

Charlotte laughed, guessing that Gervase was being deliberately amusing in order to allay their fears. There was no denying she *was* afraid, although she tried not to show it to Rebecca. The thunderstorm was certainly the worst she had ever experienced. The sky was almost as dark as night. A wind sprang up suddenly. The trees strained against its onslaught. The rain poured down as if all the floodgates of heaven had been opened.

"It is fortunate we did not ride to Tiverton," Gervase remarked lightly. But Charlotte could see that he, too, was shaken by the force of the storm.

At last it seemed to be moving away.

"I think I will take another look round," Gervase said.

"But it is so very wet," Charlotte protested. "At least put on your boots, and a thicker coat."

He smiled at her fondly. "If you say so . . ."

"Let us go upstairs," Charlotte suggested to Rebecca. "We can see more from the upper windows. The garden will be quite ruined, I should think, and the river is rising."

"There will be floods, I expect," the girl said. "When there are, the water meadows look just like a lake from my home. Sophia will certainly not come for me now," she added, with satisfaction.

Charlotte paused on the staircase. "Your sister was going to Lady Ransom's house. How far away is that?"

"Only a mile or so up-river. How did you know she was going there?"

"She called here. I forgot to tell you in the excitement of the storm. She came in the carriage, with the intention of taking you home. You were asleep, so she said she would collect you on her return."

Rebecca sighed. "Then I suppose I shall have to go with her. But, if she has any sense, she will wait a while. The road must be like a quagmire."

It was an hour later when Sophia arrived. Charlotte and Rebecca were drinking chocolate in the drawing-room, watching Gervase direct the garden boy who was up a ladder clearing leaves from a choked gutter. The storm had passed away and there was a wind blowing. But it was a hot wind, and the oppressive, humid atmosphere had not lifted.

The Pendleton carriage came slowly up the drive, the wheels thick with mud, the horses lathered. Gervase called up to the boy and, making sure that the ladder was secure, went around the house to the front door.

Rebecca pulled a face. "It will be a horrid drive to Highcleave. It looks as if the horses have had difficulty in getting even this far. Perhaps Sophia will decide to stay to dinner."

But when Sophia appeared, it was in Gervase's arms. He carried her into the drawing-room and laid her on the sofa."

"Fetch some brandy, Charlotte," he ordered, "and smelling salts if you have them. And, Becky, ask Mrs. Yeo to burn some feathers."

Wide-eyed the girl demanded, "What has happened to Sophia?"

"I know no more than you do," Gervase replied impatiently. "Hurry, now."

When Charlotte returned with the brandy, Sophia was leaning against Gervase's shoulder.

"Will bade me to come," she said and her voice was trembling. "I did not want to leave, but he said there was nothing I could do. He's still there, and with his bare hands . . . I wanted her to die, God forgive me. But not like this, not like this."

She looked up at Charlotte, who was handing Gervase a glass, as if she did not recognise her. She pushed the glass aside.

"I've had brandy already, too much. I didn't want to come away, but Will made me. He put me in the carriage and then went back—there."

Charlotte, catching Gervase's eye, raised her eyebrows. He shook his head in perplexity.

"Sophia, try to tell us, more calmly."

"*Calmly!* You expect me to be calm, after what I've been through?" Noticing her sister, hesitating in the doorway, she said vehemently, "I don't want Rebecca here. Send her away."

She leaned against Gervase's shoulder and closed her eyes. Her face was contorted. She began to talk in a different tone, without expression.

"I was sitting with Sarah Ransom in her bedroom, telling her the latest gossip, when we heard the first clap of thunder. Will was down by the river, directing the men at their digging. Sarah has always been nervous of thunderstorms, so I promised to stay with her until it was over. When it came nearer, she asked me to close the window shutters. As I did so, I saw that Will was still on the river bank. I said, 'How like him, not to bother one whit about getting wet.' And Sarah said, 'But it is so dangerous down there, under those trees. Go and find someone to fetch him in.'" Sophia buried her face in her hands. Her next words were thickened by sobs. "And so I left her." Again, she pulled herself together. "I was at the back of the house, speaking to a groom when there was a blinding flash of lightning, then . . . At first we thought the noise was thunder. But it went on and on, a kind of crashing and rumbling, and . . ." She sat up. Her shoulders were hunched, her fingers agitatedly pleating her skirt. "The whole north wing of the house was gone, Gervase. And with it —Sarah's bedroom."

"Great heaven!" he exclaimed in horror. "Are you trying to tell me that there is no—no hope of finding her?"

"Will said there might be a hollow place, perhaps, between the fallen masonry, where she could be lying, injured. They are all there digging, every man that he could muster." She turned to face him, her eyes looking huge in her pale face. "Do you not see, Gervase? If Sarah had not sent me away, I would be there, too. She was afraid of the storm, but she was thinking of Will. That was why she sent me—*me*, of all people."

Gervase stood up. "I will go, Sophia, and take Thomas and Benedict with me. But first, I insist that you drink the brandy, and then Charlotte will bring you a rug and you must lie here quietly."

"How do you suppose I can do that?" she demanded shrilly. "It was bad enough not being allowed to stay, but I am not . . . Oh, very well, give me the glass. What does it matter if I become drunk? I scarcely know now what I am saying."

She drank too quickly, the brandy catching her throat. When she recovered, she lay back, exhausted. Closing her eyes, she said wearily, "Do what you can, Gervase, though I think I know in my heart there is little hope. If Sarah is dead, William will be free. But, as heaven is my witness, I would not have had her go like this. We shall live with a nightmare all the rest of our lives."

Charlotte fetched a rug and offered to stay with Sophia. But she would have no one with her, not even her sister. Staying near at hand in case she should be needed, Charlotte could hear, through the closed door, the older woman pacing up and down, muttering to herself, half-sobbing. Rebecca, told only that the Ransom's house had been struck by lightning and help was needed, was with Mrs. Yeo in the kitchen. The house seemed strangely quiet after the turmoil of the storm. The dogs had ceased to bark, the stables were empty.

Gervase had taken even the carriage animals in case they could assist in clearing timber and masonry. Water still dripped from the choked gutter, for the garden boy had gone with the men. Through the open front door came the sound of the river.

The quiet was broken at last by the pounding of hooves on the drive. Hastening to the door, Charlotte was almost knocked off her feet by Sophia, who rushed out on to the terrace. Two horsemen came into view round the corner. One was Gervase, no longer immaculate. The other, scarcely recognisable under the grime which streaked his face, and without his wig, was Sir William Ransom. His big body was hunched forward; the reins dangled from his torn hands. As they reached the terrace, he looked up, and met Sophia's eyes. Charlotte turned away and went quickly into the house. Gervase joined her in the hall. She looked at him questioningly, and read the answer in his eyes. He spread his hands.

"No man could have done more than he did. But there never was any hope. I think he knew that. And Sophia."

Charlotte's throat felt constricted, the tears ran unheeded down her cheeks. Gently she took Gervase's hands and turned them palms upwards. The previous wounds had reopened, and blood ran also from fresh ones.

"For the second time your hands have been hurt, because of Sir William Ransom. This time, I hope you will let me attend to them."

He nodded, giving her a twisted smile. "Those wounds will easily mend. But for those two . . ." He glanced over his shoulder, then, sighing, went with Charlotte into the kitchen.

X

The lull in the storm was short lived. Thunder rumbled round the hills, and there was a great deal of sheet lightning. But now it was the rain which was frightening. It poured from the leaden sky in an unceasing, relentless deluge. The terrace was awash, the formal gardens submerged. Water cascaded from roofs, spurted from gutter pipes and found its way through windows and under doors.

Sir William had returned to help his men. Sophia, despite the deluge, seemed determined to reach Highcleave.

"You cannot possibly drive home in this weather," Gervase protested. "Your horses are like to founder, or your carriage be overturned if you attempt the hill up to Highcleave."

"Then I shall walk the rest of the way." She confronted him in the hall, hands clenched, with all her usual defiance. "Nothing you say will stop me. In any case, you no longer have the right. While Sarah Ransom lived, I could not have Will for myself. Now I can. And you may count yourself free of me. I pray you spare me any false display of regret." She turned at the door and, glancing at Charlotte, laughed shortly. "I wonder, Miss Endacott, if you would not consider Gervase a better match than your American. But take care how you manage the affair. Mr. Standish is like to have a fiery temper when roused, I think."

Gervase caught her arm. "Whether you wish it or not, Sophia, I shall accompany you. If you will wait until I . . ."

"I have no intention of waiting, even five minutes.

If I delay any longer, the road will certainly be impass-able."

Sophia pulled her hood over her head and made a dash for her carriage. Her footman's livery was saturated, his wig dripping water, as he pulled away the steps and slammed the door. Reluctantly the horses strained against the harness and moved heavily forward, with the coachman hunched miserably on his box.

Rebecca appeared from the library.

"I am thankful Sophia did not remember I was here, or she would have insisted I accompany her. Gervase, you are not going after her, surely?"

He nodded resignedly. "I must. But a pest on Sophia for her obstinacy." He smiled at Charlotte. "At least, it means you will not have to endure her barbs any longer."

"I would prefer that to your venturing out in this storm."

"Oh, we are well used to rain in Devon. With any luck, I should be back within the hour."

Charlotte and Rebecca stood at the drawing-room window as Gervase rode past. He crouched low in the saddle, his caped coat up to his ears, his hat rammed on his head at a most unfashionable angle.

When he was out of sight, Rebecca turned to Charlotte. "What shall we do, ma'am, to pass the time while we wait? I pray you, do not suggest French verbs."

Charlotte laughed. "That is most unlikely." She walked across the room. "I believe this is a spinet. Do you play, Rebecca?"

"Sometimes."

"Will you play for me now—that is, if you are feeling well enough?"

Rebecca frowned. "You need not keep fussing over me. My chest does not feel so tight now the air is fresher. Yes, I will play for you—on one condition."

"What is that?"

The girl stood with her back to the instrument and

thrust up her chin. "That you write to Mr. Standish, ending your betrothal."

Charlotte caught her breath. "You know I can do no such thing."

"Why not? You do not love him. You love Gervase, and now that he is free . . ."

"I have given my promise. I cannot break it."

"Sophia has just broken hers," Rebecca pointed out.

"I am not Sophia," Charlotte said wearily. "Besides, my promise was given willingly."

"And much too quickly. You might at least have waited a while, as Sophia was waiting, hoping that Lady Ransom would die."

"Rebecca, you must not talk like that. It is a dreadful idea."

The girl changed her tactics. She moved to Charlotte's side and tucked her arm in Charlotte's.

"Forgive me, ma'am, but you know how difficult it is for me to curb my tongue. I only want what is best for Gervase—for you and Gervase."

"If that were true," Charlotte said sadly, "you would not wish me to do what Gervase himself would not approve—break my promise to a man who has shown me nothing but kindness when I most needed it. He . . ."

She broke off, listening. Rebecca released her arm and ran to the window.

"There is a horseman coming up the drive. It surely cannot be Gervase back already."

Charlotte joined her, and at sight of the man who cantered on to the terrace, drew in her breath.

"It is John!" she exclaimed in dismay. "It is Mr. Standish."

He would come no further than the hall, for his coat was dripping, his boots thick with mud. His tricorne, when he took it off, spurted water over the apron of the maid who had answered his knock.

Charlotte asked anxiously, "John, what brings you here on such a day?"

"I was concerned about you."

"But why?" Then, before he could answer, she said unthinkingly, "Gervase was here."

He frowned. "Word was coming into Tiverton of the damage done by the storm. There was talk of a house being struck by lightning, a house standing beside the river, not far from a bridge. I could not rest until I knew . . ."

Rebecca spoke from the drawing-room doorway. "It was Sir William Ransom's house. Lady Ransom was killed. That means my sister Sophia will marry Sir William when she is able, and Gervase will be free."

"Rebecca," Charlotte said warningly.

Ignoring her, the girl came forward and faced John. "He will be free, Mr. Standish, to marry the woman he loves. And do you know who that is?"

Charlotte grasped the girl's arm. "Rebecca, that is enough. Go upstairs to your room."

For a moment Rebecca defied her, trying to stare her out. Then, reluctantly, she lowered her eyes and turned away. Slowly, with bent head and drooping shoulders, she went up the stairs.

"What did she mean?" John demanded.

"It is of no importance," Charlotte answered hurriedly. "She is a child with a wayward tongue and talks a deal of nonsense. Though it is perfectly true about Lady Ransom. John, take off your coat and come into the library and let me get you some wine."

Shrugging, he flung off his heavy greatcoat and tried to scrape some of the mud from his boots. In the library, drinking the madeira she poured, he asked, "Where is Endacott?"

When she told him, he said, "I doubt they will reach Highcleave. I had to make a detour to get here. The road is under water in several places and there is a heavy wagon overturned and blocking it about a mile beyond the bridge. If this rain continues, there are like to be floods, I think. The boys at Blundell's School hope that will happen, for they are given time off from their lessons to assist in rescuing people trapped by the Loman River."

Charlotte noticed, as she had on the day he rescued her in Tiverton, that his tone was almost indifferent. He accepted a second glass of wine.

"I surmise Endacott will be anxious about his cottages if the Exe rises much higher."

"He will be anxious about the occupants," Charlotte said tartly, and regretted her words at once as she saw the quick drawing together of John's dark brows.

Deliberately he put down his glass and faced her. "Charlotte, I begin to notice a change in you."

"Why, yes, I expect you do," she said with artificial brightness. "I am so much better in health and am quite recovered from the low spirits you saw me in on board ship."

"I did not mean that," he said and took hold of her wrist.

She felt the colour flooding into her cheeks. "How good it was of you to ride out from Tiverton in this dreadful weather, just to make sure I was safe. I am greatly touched, John, believe me, and . . ."

"Charlotte." He took her by the shoulders.

Helplessly she tried to turn away, to avoid his eyes. She longed to say, "Yes, I have changed. I no longer want to marry you." But she could not. Especially now, when he had braved the storm on her behalf; when he had again shown his thought for her welfare.

To her great relief, she heard horses approaching and glanced towards the window.

"Oh, look, here are Thomas and Benedict. Let us go and enquire if they have any more news of what happened to Lady Ransom."

For a moment it seemed that he would detain her. Then, shrugging, he let go of her wrist.

"Very well. But I shall still wish to speak to you on this matter."

She stood under the shelter of the portico as the two men rode on to the terrace. They halted at sight of her. Tom wiped his wet face on his sleeve, leaving streaks of mud.

"Mr. Gervase sent us back for a wagon, ma'am. The river is rising fast and he's afeared for the cottages. He's sending any folks up here as are willing to come, and we're to load what goods we can and stow them in the big barn until the weather eases. He's down there now, trying to persuade two old women 'tis the best thing for them."

"But I thought Mr. Gervase had gone with Miss Pendleton," Charlotte said.

"He was going with her, but when he saw what was happening by the weir, he decided he was needed there instead. After all, as the master said, Miss Pendleton has two servants to aid her. And what *I* say is, if her carriage gets overturned or washed away, 'tis her own fault for being so . . . Begging your pardon, ma'am, but you know how my tongue allus runs away with me."

"Is there something I can do?" Charlotte asked.

"Yes, ma'am," Tom answered as Benedict rode on to the stable yard, leading the carriage horses. "Mr. Gervase said as to ask you to tell Mrs. Yeo to have beds prepared on the top floor for women and children. He reckons all the men will be needed to build up the bank. 'Tis likely the floods will be as bad as they've ever had them hereabouts on account of the rain that's already fallen up on Exmoor. One of the pack-horse bridges has been swept away by all accounts and any amount of damage done and cattle lost. Why, I myself saw two dead sheep and a . . ."

"That will do, Thomas," Charlotte said. "You had best get back to help Mr. Gervase as quickly as you can."

He touched his hat and followed Benedict to the shed where the wagon was kept. As Charlotte turned indoors, she saw that John was putting on his coat.

"I will go down and see what help I can give," he

said. "If protection is needed for those cottages, doubtless I shall know better how to build a barrier than Endacott."

As he strode past her, Charlotte caught at his arm. "Tell Gervase . . ."

He paused and looked at her with raised eyebrows. But there was an expression on his face which daunted her.

"It does not matter. Take care, both of you."

He gave her a long, searching look; then, without a word, went out into the rain and mounted his horse and cantered down the drive.

Charlotte went into the kitchen to find Mrs. Yeo. She wanted to help in the preparation of the bedrooms, but the housekeeper would not hear of it.

"As if there aren't enough maids to do that, ma'am. Though, to be sure, 'tis a strange task to be putting them to. This house has never, afore now, given shelter to those who needed it. But I reckon if 'tis what the master wants, then we'd best make haste to prepare for them."

"I must do something," Charlotte insisted.

Mrs. Yeo's tone changed. "Your turn will come, ma'am, when the women and children arrive. They'll feel lost, like you did at first, and 'tis my opinion you could put them at their ease, just as if you were mistress here. 'Tis what Mr. Gervase would want, I'm sure."

Charlotte bit her lip. But for her promise to John, she could be mistress here. She could bring warmth and love into this house. She could give Gervase children, who would run and skip along the dim passages and fill the big rooms with laughter. If only she had been less impulsive, if only she had waited, as Rebecca had said.

She wandered from room to room, wondering what was happening down at the village. And suddenly she knew what she must do. Women brought up as she had been did not wait at home while their menfolk braved danger in helping their neighbours. They went out, in all weathers, and gave of themselves in whatever way they could.

Charlotte ran across the hall and upstairs to her bedroom. Hastily she found her cloak and flung it around her shoulders, pulling the hood over her head. She was changing her shoes when Rebecca appeared in the doorway.

"You are not going out, surely?" the girl demanded. Then, with dismay in her eyes, she gripped Charlotte's arm. "You are running away with Mr. Standish." She took Charlotte's arm. "I will not let you. Do you hear?"

Charlotte said impatiently, "Mr. Standish has gone to the village to help Gervase. And that is where I am going, too, in the wagon. I may be needed there."

The girl looked searchingly into her face. "Is that the truth?"

"Yes. Now let me go."

Rebecca thrust up her head. "I am coming, too."

Gently Charlotte took the girl's face between her hands. "No, dear. It is no place for you. You would get cold and wet and then your chest . . ." Seeing the disappointment on Rebecca's face, she added quickly, "Perhaps you could find some toys with which to amuse the children when they arrive. That would be most helpful."

"Very well," Rebecca agreed reluctantly. "If that is what you wish. There are some toys, I think, tucked away in the schoolroom cupboards. And there is *your* doll, the one you said you were going to give to a village child."

Impulsively Charlotte stretched out her hand towards the drawer where the doll lay. Then, abruptly, she turned and made for the door.

"I have changed my mind, Becky. I shall keep the Spanish doll, just as the—the person who gave it to me, wished me to do. I think I can never part with it, not now."

The wheels of the wagon creaked. The rain beat a continuous tattoo on the canvas roof. Through the front flap, Charlotte could see the hunched backs of Tom and Benedict, the coachman's livery looking incongruous as he drove the carriage horses between the shafts of the huge wagon which smelt of old hay, turnips and sacking.

To Charlotte they were familiar smells and she was more used to sitting, as now, on an upturned barrel than on the leather-covered seats of Gervase's carriage. If she closed her eyes, she could believe herself back in Maine, save that there was neither smell nor sound of the sea. The lassitude of the morning had left her. She felt fully alive, filled with a sense of excitement and oddly happy.

There was no reason for her happiness. Heartache lay ahead, when she must leave Gervase and Stokeleigh and go with John. But that time had not yet come. Meanwhile, there was a task to be carried out, a need for her hands and head and heart. And in helping the villagers, she would be helping Gervase.

Benedict shouted to the horses. The wagon creaked to a halt. Tom came round to the back and helped Charlotte down. All about her was noise and seeming confusion. Men ran back and forth with spades, branches cut from trees, stones and clods of turf, piling them along the river bank in front of the row of cottages. The women were huddled in their doorways, shawls about their shoulders, white-faced children clinging to their skirts. The river was a dirty brown torrent, running swiftly between the solid pillars of the bridge, foaming over the weir, carrying with it branches and leaves, long strands of grass and reeds, some broken crates, a dead hen.

Charlotte caught sight of Gervase amongst the men. He was giving orders, but she could not hear his voice above the noise of the river and the rain. He was covered in mud from head to foot. Bareheaded, his fair hair was plastered against his cheeks. Certainly he did not look elegant now, but his movements were as unhurried as ever. And there was about him an air of authority, a strength of purpose equal to John's, and Charlotte saw that the villagers were doing his bidding at once.

As she watched, John joined him. The two men stood talking for a few minutes, John gesticulating vehemently. Then he, too, went to where Gervase was pointing, and began to heave part of a tree trunk to the edge of the river bank where the water rushed, foaming, only a few inches below.

As she went towards the cottages, Gervase saw her. Before he could make any protest, she said, "It is no use your arguing. I had to come. How can I best be of use?"

"There is one old woman who will not leave," he told her. "See what you can do to persuade her. We may save the cottages, but the ground floors will amost certainly be flooded. The digging done by Ransom's men has already changed the river's course. The full force of the water is coming straight on to this bank now. It's a race against time."

She nodded and, under cover of her cloak, touched his hand. "Take care, my love."

Tom and Benedict were carrying children to the wagon, while a young mother followed, laden with an assortment of household goods. Charlotte saw Mrs. Thomson in her doorway, looking fearfully at the rising, turbulent water. Charlotte went to them.

"Everything is ready for you at Stokeleigh. Lucy, you are going to have a ride in the wagon. Come, let me carry you."

She picked up the child who clasped her arms tightly around Charlotte's neck.

"I don't like the water," Lucy complained. "Will Pa be drownded like the other man?"

"No, of course not," Charlotte assured her. "Nobody will be drowned."

" 'Tis to be hoped not," Mrs. Thomson said fervently. "The river is greedy hereabouts, and it's taken the rich as well as the poor."

Charlotte glanced towards Gervase. She wondered if, in the midst of this emergency, he was remembering his brothers and how the river had claimed them both at this point.

She saw Mrs. Thomson safely to the wagon and handed Lucy up to her. Then she returned to the cottages, squelching along the muddy path, the rain soaking through her cloak. In the third cottage she found an old woman, with a tattered shawl over her head and shoulders, huddled before the embers of a dying fire. Charlotte knelt beside the chair and took the old woman's hands in her own.

"Come with me," she urged. "Let me take you to Stokeleigh. You will be welcome there, and . . ."

The crone raised her head. Her black eyes glared at Charlotte.

"The likes of us bain't never been wecolme at Stokeleigh. They women be vüles to go there."

"But you cannot stay here," Charlotte protested. "The river is rising fast."

"I've had water through my kitchen afore now, and come to no harm. I came here as a bride nigh on fifty years agone and nobody's going to make me shift on account of a few inches of water."

"It will be more than a few inches," Charlotte warned her. "The course of the river has been changed."

The old woman pulled her hands away. "And what do you know about that, 'foreigner' that you be?"

Charlotte sat back on her heels, defeated. Then, glancing round the tiny room, she had an idea.

"Have you any food in the house?" she asked.

The old woman darted a quick glance at her. Her lips began to work.

"What's that to you?"

"There is plenty of food at Stokeleigh," Charlotte said persuasively. "Bread with butter on it and steaming hot soup. You can sit in front of the big fire in the kitchen range and smell the bread baking."

"Ale?" the old woman broke in. "Can I have a mug of ale?"

"As much as you wish."

The old woman was silent for a few moments, staring into the miserable remnants of fire. Then, stiffly, she rose and pulled her shawl more closely about her shoulders.

"All right, then, I'll come with 'ee." She wagged an admonishing finger at Charlotte. "Though, 'tis not on account of being afeared of a drop of water, I'll have 'ee know. But 'tis a pity to let all that food go to waste."

Charlotte offered an arm, but the crone would have none of that. She went to the dresser, and glancing over her shoulder, furtively lifted a china jug. Something rattled inside it and Charlotte, guessing that the old woman was anxious to take with her the only money she possessed, turned towards the door, pretending not to notice.

Gervase was just outside. His eyes lit up as he learned that Charlotte had succeeded in her persuasion.

"I thought we should have had to remove her by force," he said in Charlotte's ear. "I ought to have known that you would get your way." He caught hold of her hands. "Charlotte, how can I let you go? Seeing you like this, knowing what I could do with you beside me ..."

Warningly, she pressed his fingers. Over his shoulder she had seen John. And John was staring at them. His dark brows were drawn together. His mouth was a tight, determined line.

Charlotte said helplessly, "It is no use, Gervase. I will go back to Stokeleigh now and look after these women and children. That is all I can do for you, now or at any time."

He let go of her hands and stepped aside. The expression in his eyes caught at her heart.

John turned away. As he did so, he collided with a man carrying two buckets of stones suspended from a yoke. One bucket swung forward, catching John behind his knees. Knocked off balance, he staggered forward, and slipped on the muddy bank. In a welter of stones and turves and branches, he went over the edge.

A woman screamed. Men shouted. But Charlotte could not utter a sound. She could only stare in horror at the place where John had disappeared, and at the river, which had claimed so many lives. She heard Gervase give a kind of strangled gasp. Then he ran forward.

"Gervase, no!" Charlotte exclaimed, and clutched at his coat.

But he was already flinging it off and she stood helplessly, holding the coat, as Gervase, dodging the men who tried to hold him back, plunged into the foaming river.

Charlotte raised her head and looked dazedly around the kitchen at Stokeleigh. There was an arm about her shoulders, and a glass being held to her lips.

"Come along now, ma'am, take a sip of brandy." Mrs. Yeo's voice seemed to come from a long way off.

Charlotte's teeth chattered against the glass, but she managed to drink some of the spirit. Her hands were trembling, and she shivered violently.

"Now you'd best get out of those wet clothes before you catch your death of cold."

At the word "death" Charlotte sat upright and clutched at Mrs. Yeo's arm. "Mr. Gervase and John—Mr. Standish. They were in the river, they . . ."

"There, there, don't take on so. They're quite safe, both of them, though 'tis a miracle by all accounts."

Charlotte stared up into the housekeeper's face. "Are you telling me the truth? You are not saying this to—to comfort me?"

Mrs. Yeo shook her head vehemently. "Indeed I'm

not. If you don't believe *me,* here's Thomas who saw it all, and brought you back here."

The young footman, dripping wet, was standing in the kitchen doorway. "I'm proper thankful you've come to, ma'am," he said, as he wrung out his wig over a bucket. "I was beginning to think you'd never come out of your faint."

"What happened?" Charlotte asked weakly. "After Mr. Gervase dived into the river, I—I could not bear to look."

"I don't wonder at that," Tom said fervently. "All of us thought both gennulmen would be drowned without a doubt. But Mr. Gervase managed somehow to grab hold of Mr. Standish, then he let the current carry them on, until us could get a rope to them and drag them to the bank." He made a face as he pulled the damp wig over his cropped hair. "The master has his odd ways at times, but after what I saw him do today, he's my man for as long as he needs me."

"Where is he now?" Charlotte asked. "And Mr. Standish?"

"They just came in, ma'am, and went upstairs to get into dry clothes. When we got Mr. Gervase to the bank, he took one look at you and bade me ride back with you at once."

"I am ashamed to have fainted. I am not usually given to such weakness."

Mrs. Yeo said tartly, " 'Tis no wonder you did, ma'am. For nobody in this house has given a thought to food since breakfast. All these hours without a bite, and then to go out in this weather . . . And you're but a slip of a girl, begging your pardon, ma'am, for all your independent ways. Come now, finish this brandy, 'twill stop the shivering. And as soon as you and the gentlemen have dry clothes on, I'll serve up some hot soup."

Obediently Charlotte drained the glass, then leaned her head against the housekeeper's chest. Mrs. Yeo's roughened hand stroked her hair. Charlotte closed her eyes, and it seemed as if Bella had come back to comfort her. She felt greatly in need of comfort, for the scene of the river bank was imprinted on her inward vision. She saw again John falling into that swift-running, turbulent water, and Gervase plunging in after him. She began to tremble again, and held tightly to Mrs. Yeo's arm.

"Come now, ma'am," the housekeeper said briskly. "Let me take you upstairs. And Thomas, you'd best off with those filthy boots and go up to help the gentlemen. I reckon you'll need to find one of the late master's suits to fit Mr. Standish, for he's a deal broader than Mr. Gervase."

It could well have been Bella who helped Charlotte to undress, found fresh linen and buttoned her blue woollen gown. It could have been her beloved old nurse, and not Gervase's housekeeper, who rubbed her hair dry and gently combed it. Mrs. Yeo's solicitude only increased Charlotte's hurt. For she saw again how life might have been had she been able to remain at Stokeleigh. Everything now was changed and in so short a time. Gervase loved her, needed her. She would have been gladly accepted as mistress here, welcomed by the village, even approved by Becky. If only she had waited.

As they sat round the dining-table, the two men, Becky and herself, Charlotte thought she had rarely endured a more embarrassing meal. Gervase, looking pale and strained, made polite conversation. Becky asked endless questions. John was unusually silent. Charlotte herself, still suffering from shock, could not stop trembling, though she strove to hide it.

Gervase said, "You will of course remain here tonight, Standish. There is little chance of reaching Tiverton by road."

John thrust out his chin. "I am not the man to be put off by bad weather. As soon as my clothes are dry enough, I shall return to my lodgings." He paused, then added, "And begin my packing."

"Your packing?" Charlotte repeated in astonishment.

He looked straight at her. "Yes. My work in Tiverton is completed, and it is obvious no start can be made on the cottages here until the weather improves. I consider my duty now is to go to London, as I first intended."

Charlotte bent her head, recalling that she had been the reason for this change of plan. She wondered if he would suggest that she should go with him. If he should ask her to do so, in front of Gervase and Becky, what could she answer?

As if reading her thoughts, Gervase rose. "If you will excuse me, I think I should make sure that all the women and children have been made comfortable. Becky, will you come with me?"

For a moment the girl hesitated, and Charlotte held her breath, afraid of what Rebecca would blurt out. Then, reluctantly, she rose also, bobbed an unexpected curtsy to Charlotte, and went with Gervase.

John drained his wine glass. "Your guardian is the essence of tact."

Nervously Charlotte rolled up her napkin, and waited for what he would say next.

He pushed back his chair. "Endacott is also an exceedingly brave man. You have doubtless heard that but for his rash action, I should have been drowned?"

"Yes, I heard that," she said quietly.

"Then it can be said I owe him a great debt, the greatest debt of all. And as a man of honour, I intend to pay it in the only way I can."

She looked up. He was rubbing a hand across his forehead. He seemed suddenly younger, a little uncertain.

She said, "Gervase would not wish you to feel under any obligation to him, John. He will be only too thankful that he was able to prevent another tragedy where so many have happened before."

He raised his head. "By saving the life of the man who is to marry the woman he loves? That action was not only courageous, it was altruistic in the extreme. When I saw you both, in the doorway of the cottage . . ."

"I am sorry," Charlotte broke in. "I—I hadn't meant you to know, but now it seems useless to deny what you have guessed. Besides, I am not good at lying. But, John, I beg you to believe, I will be faithful to you. I will put Gervase from my mind and go with you . . ."

He rose and came to stand beside her. The black suit which had been Gervase's father's fitted him tolerably well, and for a moment she saw him as he would be in middle-age, standing with feet apart, shoulders back, head high.

"Is that what you think I want?" he demanded. "To play second fiddle? I thought you knew me better than that, Charlotte. You are in love with Endacott, and he with you, 'tis obvious. Just now I tried to persuade myself, and you, that I was about to behave as chivalrously as Endacott; that I would give you up as though it broke my heart to do so. But I am not the kind of man whose heart is broken by a woman. You shattered my pride, and that angered me beyond measure. But my work is the most important thing in *my* life. I know that now, and I think you knew it, too."

Slowly Charlotte rose to her feet. "Are you saying, John . . . ?"

"That I do not hold you to your promise to marry me? Yes, that is what I am saying."

She took a deep breath and looked up at him. "I am sorry, John," she said again. "I had no wish to hurt you. You have been so very kind, so understanding. You were there when I needed you."

"And you no longer do?" For a moment she saw the hurt in his eyes. Then he thrust up his chin. "But America will need me. That is where my path lies, and it is not your path, Charlotte, not any more." He turned towards the door. "And now, I surmise, my own clothes will be dry enough to put on."

"You are determined to go?"

"Oh yes. Endacott has my plans for his new cottages. It is really too trivial a task to detain me here any longer."

"Shall I—not see you again, John?"

He shrugged. "It seems unlikely."

"Then . . ." She laid a hand on his sleeve. "With all my heart I wish you well, John. That you will make good, I have not the slightest doubt. But I hope you will be happy, also, for you have made me wonderfully so."

He raised her hand to his lips, gave her a brief smile and left her. She waited a few minutes, then went into the library and sat in one of the big leather chairs. It had been so long a day. So much had happened that she had lost track of time. It was almost dark outside, but the rain had eased off a little. A fire had been lit and the flames crackled softly. The clock on the mantelpiece ticked away the minutes until Gervase should come.

She laid her head against the chair back and closed her eyes. She felt a great weariness take hold of her, as if she were drained of all strength. She let her thoughts drift. They were no longer troubled, but full of thankfulness and hope.

She did not even hear the door open. But she opened her eyes to find Gervase kneeling beside her. He took her hands in his.

"Standish has just gone," he said quietly. "He said very little, but I guessed . . ."

Charlotte sat forward. "I am free, Gervase, just as you are."

Gervase smiled and shook his head. "No, my love, neither of us is free, not any more. We belong to each other, for the rest of our lives."

She laid her head on his shoulder. He put his arms

about her and kissed her. And she knew that what he said was true, she would belong to Gervase all the rest of her days; to Gervase and to Stokeleigh.

5